REMINGTON

QUEEN'S BIRDS OF PREY BOOK 5

KATHI S. BARTON

This is a work of fiction. Names, characters, places, and incidents are products of the author's imagination or are used fictitiously and are not to be construed as real. Any resemblance to actual events, locations, organizations, or persons, living or dead, is entirely coincidental.

World Castle Publishing, LLC
Pensacola, Florida
Copyright © Kathi S. Barton 2021
Paperback ISBN: 9781955086301
eBook ISBN: 9781955086318
First Edition World Castle Publishing, LLC, June 7, 2021
http://www.worldcastlepublishing.com
Licensing Notes
Cover: Karen Fuller
Editor: Maxine Bringenberg

Prologue

The castle was going down, thanks wholly to her birds. Queen Dante sat upon her horse and watched as stone after stone crumbled to the ground. In a matter of moments, not only were the walls of the fort destroyed, but the king inside his castle was dead as well. Turning her mount, she headed back to the encampment to ready herself for the long ride home. The birds joined her not half an hour later, their large bodies covered in dust and blood.

"You have done well, my darlings." They could understand her and she them, but no one else could. She had made them what they were, and she would be the only one to control them.

"Have you fed well on his dying cattle? What serves a man to have his food dying? His people, they were fed no better, I saw."

The falcon—she had never named them—told her the people were headed west. In a few months, probably less, they would all be dead too. It bothered them when the people suffered because of the king or queen of the castle. But it was to be. Dante could not care for anymore in her own keep.

No one would attack her keep. If they tried, she knew them to be too stupid or too drunk on their own mead. She had her birds, all of them bigger than life, made large by magic that she gave them. Looking at them as they landed around her, forever keeping her safe, she wondered why she had not thought of it sooner when her king was still alive.

"I would have set you upon him. You could have eaten him for your dinner. Though I suspect it would have given you a great deal of belly pains." The hawk told her she was lucky he had died the way he had. No one would come for her if she had killed him. "Yes, that is very true. But I suffered greatly when he was living. No children either, to give me comfort in my olden age. Though they might have been just like him, and that would have been too much to bear."

She would never marry again. Love wasn't anything she searched for. Not that she didn't have someone to warm her bed on occasion, but it was nice to be able to send them on their way when she had finished with them. Her heart belonged to no one, and she would not have another man take her to bed by force. All would be well, and no one would threaten to come and take over her home. That was a certainty.

The hawk used her beak to put delicate things upon the backs of the others. There was aplenty this time. Barrels and smoked meats. Pottery that they would use like it wasn't worth a king's gold. They raided the castle each time they conquered. Hawk was the best at getting in and out before they took the place to the grounds.

The eagle took off toward home. She would let the people know the queen was returning simply by showing up. They would have a feast this night. The food upon her back would feed them for many days, and the barrels of spices, hoarded in the lower levels of the castle, would go a long way toward helping them trade for what they did not grow.

The phoenix, by far the deadliest of her birds, shed her feathers in anticipation of getting new ones. After a battle, she would become anew, each time getting stronger, and her feathers, brilliant now, would be brighter still. She could flame a fire so hot that stone would crumble under a man's feet. The ground would no longer hold a seed within its belly to produce food, and she could kill a man with a single breath so that there would be nothing left of his body.

She loaded the last of her things onto the back of the owl. She might be small, she had always thought, but she could carry more than her own weight. And she would pick up her horse, used to flying through the sky like a bird himself, and take him back to the castle. He would be fed and groomed before the queen ever landed on the ground.

The vulture squawked at her, and she turned to look at the two men there. They looked as if they might have been about to kill her, but the sight of such large birds threw them off their duty. In no time at all, the vulture snapped both of them up and ate them down. A gruesome sight, but one that filled her heart with joy too. She was safe again. The vulture took off, too, once she was loaded up.

"Well, my falcon, it is just you and I left." She told her she was still armed. "Yes, well, probably not too bad of an idea seeing that they nearly shot us."

The falcon laid her body to the ground. She was the only one fitted with a seat, one that Dante rode on. Scouring the area, Dante always made sure the places she camped were left as neat and clean as she'd found them. Sometimes in better shape. As she climbed on the back of her bird, she held her breath.

"I do hate the height. I should have thought this through when I turned you into my warriors." Her laugher, should there have been someone around to hear it, might have caused them to think her insane. "Homeward, my love, and we shall eat well tonight."

She took no one with her on her fights except the birds. That was why she believed her people were so loyal to her. She protected them, fed them better than herself, and made sure there was plenty for them to trade and share for things that she did not provide for them.

The soil was rich and would give forth a bounty like no other gardens. Flowers, too that were woven into pretty things and traded. There was a smithy, as well as a doctor who doubled as a dentist. They had even acquired a grave digger, who also made markers.

There was a single merchant that came by, his wagon filled when he arrived, but it would be near empty when he left. The latest news came with him and any posts he had been asked to bring to them. He would also, for a small coin, take outposts for the next time he was in the keep of a relative or friend.

And today, there was such a missive. But it was for her, from someone she had hoped never to hear from again—the king of the land, the only man she answered to, though it wasn't with any kind of happiness on her part.

After the others were settled down and the food that had been brought put into storage, she sat down and wasn't surprised that the falcon came to see her. The room she was in—the throne room for lack of a better term—had no roof and six perches for the birds when they wished to see her. Otherwise, they sat upon the top of the castle turrets, watching for anything that might befall them.

"I am to wed. The king of the land, he has

decided my castle is the best there is, and he will marry me himself." The falcon asked about his castle. "He says it will be his son's, of which he has none as yet. His last five wives have only given him daughters from what I have heard, and they did not last long afterwards."

The falcon asked her what she would do. Dante knew what would happen to her should he come here. He would kill her. Being in her fortieth summer, she was much too old to bear any children now, and he would be better with a younger bride. One that could birth him the sons he wanted.

"He will kill me; we both know that. And you six will kill him or be killed. I worry so much for the people here too." She thought of several plans and threw them out. It was in her head that if she should die, then she would do so on her own terms. "I will need a day to think on this. In the meantime, he says he will be here in the new year. That will give us a month to provide for the people and make sure they are not harmed."

~*~

Dante worked as hard as the rest of her people. With her hair up in a rag, she didn't look any different than any of the men and women that toiled with her. There was much to be done in the little time they'd been allotted. Today they were drying all the beef and goat meat they had. It would last them for several months, and where she was sending them for safety, they'd need that extra time. Long enough for them to breed more of their cattle and goats, so there would always be food for them to eat.

"What of the dried herbs that are left, my lady? There are already barrels of it packed away for the trip. Shall we put them in bags to go?" She shook her head. "There are no more barrels until the morn. The copper is working as fast as he can, making more. What shall we do?"

"Leave them. There is very little, correct?" The man said that there wasn't enough for a good strong stew. "Good. They will think you all died off from lack of planning, and that will keep you safe for a longer time. Leave it for them so that when the keep and castle are in ruin, the king will understand why."

Not that anyone was going to be coming to the castle to live, she thought. There were things in motion that would make sure everything here was gone well before the lands were walked upon again.

She looked to the sky when a dark shadow fell over her. Her hawk was making her way to the village Dante had set up. Long ago, Dante had purchased the lands far from where she was now and put them in the name of Mercy Dante. She knew so much about all their futures that it made her so sad to know she'd never be there to see it happen.

"My lady?" She looked at her man of arms, a man that had very little work to do but was brave and true to her. "We have plenty of things to go on the next load if you have a desire to send it on. Do you still wish for some of the armed men to go with them this time? I'm to understand we're to fell trees for homes."

"Yes, that would be good. How many men can you spare today?" He told her all she had. "Then send them on. I know some of you are frightened to ride the birds, but you should have no fear. They would no more harm you than they would me." He nodded and looked at her hawk. "I shall send you all on her. She is the gentlest of the six of them."

The carrier had been fashioned a week ago. It had upset her that it had taken so long to get right, but it was safe now, and that was all she wanted. There were only a few short weeks to get the people gone from here with all that would keep them safe. Now all she had to do was make sure the birds didn't know the last of her plans.

The platform had been made from several drawbridges from castles they'd taken over. She'd known that saving them would be helpful, but it had taken a great deal more work than she'd thought to put them together and have her fishermen weave a netting to carry it with. After several trials and failures, the carrier worked.

Loading up the men on the first run of people, she noticed they had put the several men that were afraid of the ride in the middle. One of them, a hardy man otherwise, had been knocked out with much wine. It had been funny to all around that it had taken so little of the wine to do that to him. But they didn't know she'd given him a bit of magic to help him travel. All was well when her hawk took off with the several dozen men to start on the homes that would be needed.

Barrels would be next. They had been sealed by magic that would keep them well preserved. The other birds, her warriors for all time, had been taking jewels and other items to a cave she had also covered in magic. It would help the people of the new village for as long as they lived, well beyond her body becoming nothing but dust.

Dante watched as several more people were taken to the new village. She would allow them to name their new place as long as it would never be attached to the name of the castle. That would be bad for them and would bring much trouble onto their heads. When her hawk landed, she went to ask how things were progressing.

"Well, my lady. They were no more off the platform for seconds when they started to work. I believe you were good to get them started on this. 'Tis only late winter, so they should be able to have a few of the buildings up before the rest are moved." Dante agreed with her. No one else could understand the birds but her and the other birds. It had, she knew, kept everyone safe all these years. "I can only make two trips there and back, my lady. 'Tis not a long way by the way we fly, but the pack is heavy. Please forgive me for that."

"You have nothing to be sorry for, my bird of prey. You have done one more than I had hoped for this day. And when the others have finished their tasks for me in carrying away the riches and other things they will need, it will take no time at all to move the rest. Nay, you have done well this day in taking the men and then the food to feed them while there." Her hawk, who would someday be called Blaze, bowed before her.

Stacking up the loads that would be going on the platforms, she could see that they'd be taking away the last of it only the day before the king was to arrive. Dante was glad now that she'd had such good people working for her. They asked nothing as to why they were doing this but did it for her. When in reality, it was all for them and her birds.

Dante knew the king would never make it here. His ship and all his bounty would be deep in the waters he crossed to kill her and take her castle. The man was a fool to think she would easily do what he wanted. Wiping at a tear, she looked around the keep she'd worked so hard to keep everyone safe in.

It was then she saw her son. Duncan was everything she was and more. Each time she saw her son, she would give him a little more of herself, teach him something of running a castle. He knew what he was to her and that Mary was doing her a great favor in keeping him safe. Duncan would be a greater king than she ever was a queen. Just the way it should be. She was glad now that she'd told him he was to be mated to one of her birds.

Leaving him to his work, she entered the castle to see what else was there that she could easily live without. There was very little left as it was, but she moved from room to room to make sure nothing was left behind of any value. The only thing she could see in the great room was the painting of herself.

Dante wished so many times that she could have put her son there with her, but it was not to be. It would have been foolhardy to think she'd be able to keep him safe if she was to put out there that he'd been born. Other kingdoms would have done a great many things to have captured him to bring her to heel. Dante would do anything to keep him safe, including submitting to a man again. A thing that she would never do again in her lifetime.

"I shall give this to our falcon." She turned her head enough to find Duncan behind her, and the doors closed to anyone walking around. "She will be a great person, I think. Sour to many but the one that she will love."

"You have seen this?" Duncan said he'd seen a great many things. "Well, you know as well as I that it might not turn out the way we see it. There can be changes, you know."

"This I am aware of. As well as you not living past the last person that is taken from here." She turned to look at him then, trying to see just what he was seeing. "I shall forever miss you, Mother."

It was the first time he'd called her that. Her heart was so tender of late that she would burst into tears at all that would be gone in so short of time. Hugging him to her, she felt the strength in his body was getting stronger daily. He knew how to work and did it without complaint.

"I have been writing a book. It is just for you, my son. You will know things I have known for some time. It will replenish your riches that I have put aside for you. Also, how to keep the birds safe should they need it." He nodded. "I will give it to Mary on the day you travel. I do not want the others to know you are my son, even after all is finished here."

"They will only know me as a man you trusted. But I will need to tell them at some point. This you know as well as I. I will be their king when they need me." She nodded, tears flowing quickly now. "Mother, you do know I will take care that they are as safe as you made them here?"

"I do, my son. I know that better than you could. You are not anything like your father. A cruel and terrible man. When you marry, and you will, I want you to know that she will only love you if you give her your heart. It's important that you do that for her." He said he would. "Let her strength help you when you know you are not armed to do it on your own. She will love you more and respect you forever for that."

"Will she be stronger than me, Mother?" Dante told him she was sure of it. "Then I will be for her what you have been for these people. A leader of worth. I will promise you I will also protect her forever."

"That is all that anyone can do for their mate, my child." He hugged her, something neither of them were able to do often. "I shall miss you, Duncan. Much more than I could ever explain to you. Go forth, protect all the people of your kingdom, and do what I say. Love your mate more than anyone, including yourself, and the two of you will be able to move mountains."

~*~

New Town, what they had begun to call the new place they were living, looked like any other town in the country. The only difference was, this one was only several weeks old. It, to Dante, looked as if it had been established long ago. She was pleased with the work her people had given the place she'd moved them to.

"My lady? There is a problem in one of the homes we've put up. I know how to fix it, but the man living in it, he said he will be fine with it. To have his own home was more than he could have hoped for." The queen of the people asked Barron what the issue was. "He has five daughters, my lady, and we've somehow put him into a house with only one bedroom. There are ones he could use, but he insists that it be used for the other families."

"I shall speak to him. Is it Donald, the mule man?" Barron nodded, his face nearly touching the ground, he was bent so much. "Stand up, man. I believe I have pointed out this is not a time for formality. We must all work together for the greater good of the people. I shall speak to him now. Then I must, as you know, return to the castle for the final loading."

Along the way to speak to Donald, she was stopped no less than twenty times to be thanked for the things she'd provided for the people here. Without making the great move, Dante knew all of them would have been killed. Because of their loyalty to her as queen of the castle, the king of these realms, a tyrant of a man, would have ordered them all butchered as soon as he killed her on their wedding night. Of this, she was certain.

"My lady? I have yet to put on a pot for tea, but you must join us in it." Dante was not one to hold back when she had something to say. She told Donald she wanted him to take a larger home. "Oh, my lady. Barron should never have bothered you with this. We are quite happy with where we are."

"But you have six people in a single man's home, Donald. What, I ask you, will the man who was supposed to be in this home do with a home with many bedrooms? He will be overwhelmed in trying to keep them clean while you are smashed up in this one-bedroom chamber with your little girls." Donald looked at his daughters, beautiful little ones that were the pride and joy of himself. "There is a home just over the road here you shall be moved to. I insist. Your daughters will share two bedrooms, and you will have your own. I know for a fact, sir, that your snore is legendary. For your daughters to have a good sleep, you will need to be far from them. Do you not agree?"

"Yes, my lady." He moved just a little closer, and in a low voice, spoke to her. "I did not wish to cause you any undue trouble. You have given all of us a chance to survive this, and I wanted to be sure you knew I was ever so grateful for it. I'm as happy here with you and yours as I ever was in the castle keep, my lady. Incredibly happy."

"I'm glad you're happy here, Donald. You are a good man and a man that cares well for his daughters. I shall have the men move you to the new home. It will give me a good feeling knowing you have plenty of room for yourself and your family." He thanked her. "Your daughters, sir, they will be safe here. You need anything, you make sure you contact Barron."

"Thank you, my lady. If there is ever anything I can do for you, you need only to ask. I am and will be indebted to you for the rest of my days." Dante felt her eyes water up with the man's words. Her life, she knew, was only a short time away from ending. "Thank you very much."

The little girls curtsied at her, and she had to move on. It broke her heart every time she saw small children. She so wanted to hold her own. Telling Donald once again that she'd have the men move him, she moved toward the long house that would serve as a church for the people and a meeting place for them to gather should they need to. Her eagle was awaiting her when she returned to the now all but abandoned castle.

"You have done well, my heart. You, of all the birds I have, are the one I worry most about." The eagle asked her why. "You are so much like me. Hard when you're needed to be. Too soft when it comes to our people. I fear someday it will harm you in ways that not even I could fix."

Her eagle, like the other birds, was a huge part of getting the people moved. If not for them, there would be no way she could have done this alone. It would have meant certain death for all of them, including her own son.

Going to the throne room, she sat upon the floor. Dante had moved her chair to the caves for the others to sell off should no one want it. But because she could see into the future, just bits and pieces, she knew at least one of them would want such a monstrosity.

"When this is finished, soon now, I will give you and the others magic to keep you safe from others who would try and capture you." Her eagle asked what sort of magic. "You will be able to blend into situations you wouldn't normally consider a problem. There will be problems, too. From the things I have seen, you all will have trouble from those around you."

She laid back on the cold stone. The castle had been forged so long ago, Dante could not remember who had been the person to have erected it. Now, as she looked up into the night sky, the roof here long since removed, she thought of what was going to happen in the coming days.

"He has set sail and is nearly here. The king of all the lands is coming to claim not just my castle and my wealth but my birds as well. There are many people on the vessel that carts his bottom here who have no desire to be his servants. If only I could have saved them as well." The eagle, standing upon her perch built just for her, reminded her she could not save them all. "In this, I wish it was wrong to have thought that. They will suffer, these people. They are suffering, for there is nothing to do to appease the king to find favor with him. There are so few that he has not made suffer by lashing them on their backsides. Too many of them have died in his foolishness to make me his wife for such a short time."

Listening to her eagle squawk at her about the king and idiocy, Dante thought of her impending death. It would be a sad affair only to her son and the birds he would one day claim as his own. However, just knowing all would be safe from the king's tyranny made the other things so worthwhile.

"If I had to do it again, I would do nothing differently. I would still do what I am doing now so that all will live and live on. Even with you birds, I would do just what I have done to keep my kingdom here." The eagle asked her if she'd been happy. "Happy? I don't know that I have had that much in my lifetime. I have been content. Not the same, I suppose, but I have been content with my lot in life. If only I could have kept living the way we have, I do believe I could have made such a difference in things here and in the future. Before I forget this again, I have taken the time to write out the things t'will keep the new town with coin in their coffers. I know it will be aplenty, but I will worry until my last breath if it will be enough."

Her last breath. It was only a few days away. Much too soon for her, but Dante knew it would be well worth the pain of dying to her. Sitting up, she looked at the birds, all six of them on their perches watching over her and the emptied lands they could see. They were the sole reason she was able to do this. This she knew more than anyone could have guessed.

"I shall retire, I think. I have no bed to speak of now, so I will only lie upon the ticking. On the morrow, we shall have a feast. A great amount of food, as well as drink. 'Tis fitting, I think, to celebrate this new way of life for so many." Her beautiful phoenix asked her why she seemed so sad. "Sad? Aye, I am that and more. Things are moving at a pace I wish didn't exist. But it is for the wellbeing of all that have called this place home. In that, I suppose I am sad that we shall never be able to return here in my lifetime."

But they would. All six of them and more will return someday and see the castle as it should have been. A lovely home to her son and his mate, the one that she herself had hand-picked for her beloved child. Oh, to be able to see them grow into love. But it was not to be.

Getting up before she made a fool of herself by crying over something she had no control over, Dante did indeed head to her bed. For tomorrow and the next day would be the hardest of anything she'd ever done before.

~*~

Dante didn't sleep. She'd not closed her eyes

to rest in more years than she could count on both her hands and then her toes. It was all right, she supposed. Dante was able to get more done this way. But she did pace herself. She'd never survive these last days if she were to fall apart now.

"Mistress, there are two men here to see you. They wish to know who has carved your turrets. I did not tell him they were as real as he." Mary shook her head at the folly of some men. "I should have called them down to talk to him about how they were made. I think he might well have soiled his britches."

"Mary, please tell them that the lady of the castle is busy and does not have time to tell him of the art he is looking at. What manner of person would ask such a thing? As if I didn't have the sense of that turtle caught in the drain last week. Nay, tell them to move on before I toss them into the sea." Mary went to tell them just what she said. Dante was smiling when she heard Mary laughing.

She'd no doubt take the way she'd told her to move them on to such extravagance. It would serve the men right if she really would call down one of her birds to take care that they didn't bother her again. Dante made her way to the drying room at the back of the kitchen. She had been brewing a brew for several days now.

"You're not going to be going with us, are you, my lady?" She turned to look at her great phoenix. "If you do not explain to me what your plan is, I think to tell Mercy what I have figured out. She will not allow you to die. Nor will I be all right with your death."

"I must die, my beautiful friend. For if the king were to actually reach our lands and find this castle and all that was here when he set sail were gone, what do you think he'd say to his men? That it was a good thing I left? That now he didn't have to kill me? Nay, he would send them to find me. And my people. I do not wish anyone else to be harmed for what he wants from me." The phoenix, Piper would be her name someday, asked her if she expected them to do the killing. "In a way. I have this brew here. It is nearly set for me to drink down. The castle and its walls, they must come down, or it will all be for naught. What I have made, it will have me dead before you drop the first stone upon the only home I have ever had. You as well, my dear bird."

"Mercy will not be willing to help." Dante told her she would because she'd know what she said now was the truth. "Aye, you say that, but I think her to be most upset with the turn of events, my lady. It will break all our hearts to know you have left us behind."

"I shall never leave any of you behind. I will be forever in your hearts and you in mine as I take my last breath." The phoenix nodded but didn't say anything more for some time. "He will die before he gets to the land. This king who thinks to murder me in my own bed. And those that he brought with him, they too will perish. 'Tis a folly on his part to think I'd just do as he wants as if I have no mind of my own. I know Mercy will kill him and all that have been forced to come here with him. It's not such a bad thing, these deaths, Phoenix. It will be merciful to all that have ridden the seas to make their way here."

After the bird left her, she pulled the large cauldron off the hot flames and covered it with a lid. Even though there were no children about or anyone working in the kitchens, she would feel terrible if any harm would come to anyone right now. Making her way back to the throne room, or what was left of it, she laid on the floor to look up at the sky.

Dante hated heights. While she forever

knew she'd never see the time when there would be airplanes in her sky, she knew they were set to come. She was content, for now, to bask in the beautiful view she'd miss more than she'd thought she might. Getting up, Dante made her way to the side of the castle that faced the sea.

"Oh, to see the waterways filled with my own ships again. To see them sailing off to find new things to bring back to us." There were ships out there. She could just make out their flags. None of these were her tormentor, she knew. He would be visible in two days, still out to sea a long way. He would be nothing more than a small speck in the open waters, but she'd still be able to see him. "Why now? Why have you made your plans to include me at this time? I wish more and more I'd been born a male. Then no one would dare to come here. I might well have been the king of all the lands had it been so."

Her ships had been taken to the coves not far from here. By the time they were remembered, time would go by, and they would be nothing more than rotted wood and material. Dante wouldn't want them to be seaworthy again. It might well be the thing that got her people killed. Even in the future, the bits and pieces she could see, the ships would only cause people to look harder for her remains and perhaps run into the New Town where her people lived. That, she knew, would be a danger to all.

"Mother? Are you here?" She turned to look at her son. Duncan had been coming to her of late to get more lessons, her thoughts on things, as well as how to manage a vast kingdom such as the one she was leaving him. "I thought for sure you'd be here. I have a favor to ask of you. 'Tis a small one, but one I think you can give me. I should like to spend the night here, within these walls, once with you. I have spoken to Mary about it, and she thinks you will grant me this one wish. It will be the first and last time the two of us will be able to be under the same roof since I was born."

"I should like that. Very much." He nodded and smiled at her. "There is so much to tell you and so much more I think I have forgotten to pass on to you. But for this night, I shall not speak of the king coming here. Nor of my life ending. You are aware of it, my child. This I know. But to have you here with me this last night? It is more than I could have asked for."

They made their plans to sleep on the same ticking she'd been resting on since her bed had been taken away. As they curled up under a thick blanket, the two of them talked more than they rested. Tears were shed, of course. There was no way to avoid such a thing. But there was laughter, too, much more of it than just tears.

"I shan't be here tomorrow when you are set. I cannot be of sound mind when I know what is to happen to you. I will tell you, Mother, that there couldn't have been a better person to raise me. Nor one that has loved me as well as you have." She kissed him on the forehead as he spoke again. "For as long as I live, Mother dear, I will keep you in my heart, along with the birds that will be mine as well. I love you. Much more than I think any child could their parent. You are the best there is. I shall kill anyone that says differently."

She had no words to give him after that. Her heart, already tender, was breaking more. It might well have done her better not to have spent the night with her son. But it would have been harder on her, she thought, to not have this time with him with no other around.

Finally, when she could speak without tearing up even more, Dante told her son that she loved him. That he'd be a better king than she had been a queen. After saying that, they both settled into their thoughts until the sun came rising from the seas that surrounded them.

Today, she knew, would be her last day to breathe in the air, take in food for her belly, and the very last time she'd order her birds to do something she knew they'd hate her for.

~*~

The last of the herbs were drying nicely. Along with the pumpkins and other squashes, Dante had added a little magic to them so that they'd produce quicker. Would also produce more for them to have when they replanted the seeds left from this bounty.

The corn stalks had been bundled up too to take along for roofs, as well as fodder for the fires that would need to be lit. As she looked over the ground she'd been working on with the others, she wondered if the future occupants of her home would plant and use the product coming from it as much as she had.

Dante knew a great deal about the coming centuries. It had come to her in dreams or just single thoughts. She used this gift of magic to make it so her son and all the people that were going to be living around here would not have to worry about money. Not when there was so much more that needed to be done.

Taking a large basket of still green tomatoes that hadn't gotten ripe as yet, she was smashing them into pulp to make sure that the seeds, a precious thing, were set aside to dry. Duncan joined her in the drying room with several more fruits that would need to be secured.

"I have dug up all the trees you wished to be stored away. I also added some things that seemed to be begging me for a second chance. I've a feeling in my heart that their kind might not be long for this time we are in." She told her son he was more than likely right if that was what he felt. He walked around the room. "There is plenty enough herbs here to fill an entire barrel. Are you leaving them?"

"I will some. The rest will go back with all the others when you leave here tonight." He nodded. "The trees will be stored away until such a time that they're needed. I have found a way to preserve them so they will not rot and die. I will let you know when it is time for you to get them. Also, there is—"

"Mom, I have a question for you. You do not need to answer it if you would rather not, but I would so like the answer." She nodded and sat in the only chair in the room with them. "No one will speak to me of my sire, my father. I have asked Mary, and she has told me when the time was right, I'd be able to know all there is to know about him. I believe in my heart that no one can tell me what sort of person he was but you. It's important to me, you see. I would like to know why I was hidden from him. Not that I don't believe you did the right thing. But I cannot imagine the cruelty he had without you telling me."

"It is a horrific telling, my son. One I hoped you'd never hear. But since you have asked, I will tell you of his deeds. Not just to me, but to the very people that work within and out of these walls." He sat on the floor, and Dante produced a thick ticking for him to sit on while he listened. She did the same for herself and leaned back against the tables used for the sorting of herbs. "When I was first wed to him, by order of the then king, he was cruel even then. I wasn't a young maiden, but a maiden all the same. Yet his lying with me was like lying with a monster. He hit me, bit me, and then when he'd filled me with his seed, he would have me tied to the bed so I'd not be able to abort any child from him with the taking of herbs or such. I allowed that to happen to me only the one time. After that, using my magic, I'd be free and wandering around without his knowledge."

"Did you? Abort any other children by him?" She told him she'd never have done that. Not even if she had ten children, all of them girls. "I'm glad to hear that, Mom. It would have been nice to have a sibling, but I understand that it would have been difficult to want to have a child by such a monster."

Duncan sat on her lap then, just there so that she could hold him. While sitting there with his head under her chin, she told him of the things his father had done to her. What he would have done had he ever found out about her having a son.

"There were times, my son, that I would wish for death after he was finished with me. The healers had to work very hard to keep me from throwing myself from the highest peak. The wounds I would carry during my life cut harder than any other thing I have had to endure. Even a spear, which I have had plenty enough of, were nothing compared to his terror." While not giving him a great many of the details, she did tell him of the whip he'd used. His fist, as large as her head, would slam into her body any time he saw her.

Dante told her son some of the things she

wished for him to remember. The decision was his mate's, and hers alone, as to when to have children or not. There were other things too that she imparted to him. The wisdom of keeping his mouth shut when he was angry. To not make decisions without discussing them with his mate.

"Your mate will be smart, Duncan. And stronger than you will ever be. Not just in strength but also in mind. She will have knowledge that comes from being a warrior. Use that. All the birds will be able to protect you in ways I cannot see or even imagine." He told her he'd treat his mate the opposite way from how Dante had been treated. "Then that is all that I can ask of you, Duncan. I will die knowing you will be the greatest king that has ever lived."

"I will not disappoint you or my mate, Mom. I promise you on my heart and yours that I will treat her as the queen she will be." He kissed her on the cheek. "Come with me now. I want to swim with you while the others are finishing up. One hour will make little difference in getting ready for a king that will not see this place."

The two of them played in the water for more than half the day. When they weren't swimming, the two of them talked about the things she'd seen. The companies, what they were called in the future, would make him the most profit, also about when he was to sell them so as not to lose a great fortune.

"There are things called market that are nothing like we have here. They are to buy and sell stocks—I believe that is what they're called. The things I have written for you will tell you when to buy such stocks and when to sell them. One minute will make the difference in when you sell them, Duncan. Be on time for that." He told her he would. "Good. That is all I can ask you to do. It will be able to sustain you for years and years."

As Duncan made his way home, she mixed up her tea and took it with her to the towers. Duncan thought it would be tomorrow morning, but she didn't know if she could go through with it if she knew he was standing not far from her. As she settled herself into the middle of the room, she looked up at the skies. The birds, all of them, were awaiting her signal. Drinking the brew straight down, she told her birds how much she had come to love them.

"Once I am gone from this world, which will not be long now, you will receive a gift from me that you'll need to survive under the conditions of the world beyond." She didn't tell her birds what she'd done, that she'd poisoned herself with her own brew. Nor did she tell them she'd made it so they'd be humans. Also, they'd be true immortals and not able to be killed. Dante was afraid they'd not take down the castle but leave it for others to take over. There would be no one else to live here but her sons and the birds. Even though he didn't know it yet, the castle would be ready for them to live in quite nicely.

"You are angry. I can feel it. I'd rather you be happy that the other people that were living here are as safe as we could make them. That without you, I don't know that I would have been as long for this world as I was. You not only saved the people here, my birds but me as well." Her vulture asked her why she had to die. They could carry her away. "If there is even a hint of me being not at this castle when it fell, then I will be hunted down for treason. They will not only kill me, but they'll have their sport with me, as well as torture me to find out where my people have gone. I know I cannot survive the sort of torture they would put upon my body. I am old, and my body wouldn't sustain as much as they will use against me to go and find them."

Her body was weak already from her magic being depleted as much as it was, but she held onto her mind for as long as she could. Telling her saviors about how she had known to find them. That they were, of all the birds around, the ones she knew would care for her and her lands. Telling them that it was time, well past the time, for the work to be done. Then she told them one more thing before she succumbed to her death.

"I love you all so very much. Had you been children of mine, I would have— You are my children. Created from me so that I could be a good queen to all that lived here. But I would have taken glory in your lives. Been a part of it that would have made me the happiest I have ever been. There has never been a greater friendship than the kind we have here. I do love you. Please, remember me fondly." She tried to laugh a little, but she was too weak to even do that now. "Let it begin. I shall wish you all the blessings a queen can give to her mates, best friends and children that you are."

Dante was beyond feeling anything when the first stone tore into the building. It narrowly missed her, for which she was disappointed. They were thinking she might change her mind. Even if she wished to do that, it was too late.

Her last vision was of her great vulture carrying a large stone up and over her. Dante closed her eyes, letting death take her before the stone could do so.

Chapter 1

Remi tasted the soup she was making. It was missing something, something that would make it go from blah to zappy. Looking around, she put her finger into the brew on her spoon and asked it to tell her what it was she had missed. The soup, thankfully, didn't ask questions but gave her a list of the ingredients she'd used. One time over the years, she'd asked a lobster what dish it would like to be. It had only been a question she was asking herself, but her magic had taken it to mean she wished for the large crustacean to answer her.

That had been the biggest mistake of her life around the stove. Grinning, she to this day could hear the lobster telling her he wasn't going to give her a recipe to cook him with and had snapped at her. It had chased her, literally, out of the kitchen and into the thankfully empty restaurant she'd been in. It took her several long years to get over having food speak to her.

"Lady Remi, there is a man here to see you. He said you were expecting him. I don't believe him, so you know. He seems to be quite messy if you were to ask me." She asked the host on duty what he said he wanted with her. "He wouldn't say, the turd. But I have taken it upon myself to see. He is here about the investigation you're working with."

"Yes. I know him now. Would you please send him back here? He's working on something for the other birds."

He nodded but didn't leave without telling her he wasn't going to leave her alone with the man. She wondered if he ever thought of what she'd done in the old times as her large bird.

Mr. Caldwell was nothing like what she'd expected him to be. In her mind, he was an older gentleman with balding gray hair, as well as a beer belly. She had to turn from him for a moment to get her laughter under control. He looked just like that old detective from the seventies—*Columbo,* she thought his name was. The detective was forever crumbled up looking with a hat atop his dark crew cut hair.

"I've found some information for you, Miss Remi." He handed her a thick file with the word Piper across it. "Miss Piper is out of town this week, and she asked me to come and see you. I hope that's fine."

"Yes. Piper is at a couple of shows until the end of January. This is a picture of who?" He told her. "Rosemary. I guess she goes by Rose. This picture must be her son, I'm thinking. Do you have any of the man you were looking for too?"

He flipped the file to the end and showed her a picture. He looked enough like Basil, the king of the fae, to have been thought of as his twin brother. However, where Basil was slim, Juniper looked heavier. His face was also showing some signs of overeating a little.

Basil had told them last week that since his brother wasn't in line for the throne, he didn't have the same magic as he had. He'd gain weight and age, but extremely slowly. Since he'd be in the thousands of years old, he would be looking like a man in his early seventies.

Remi looked again at the picture of Rose.

"The woman there, she doesn't go out much. I thought it was because she was hiding something, but I realized then that she was ordering things online to have delivered to her doorstep. The house is in the son's name. Sorrel Herb owns not only the house but the car as well. It took me a while to figure out that he doesn't live here at all. I had a bit of trouble finding anything about him until I spoke with Ms. Coby to get a little magic to make it appear." He laughed a little. "Do you find her to be scary?"

"All of us are scary, Mr. Caldwell." She looked at the information he'd given her. "This says they have no jobs, but they're living in a three million dollar house. Did you find any banking information on them?"

They'd had no idea what the son's name would have been. Finding out that everything, including their banking information, was in Sorrel's name would make it so Mercy or any of the other birds could make a better attempt at finding them.

"I was able to find a couple of credit card numbers, also in the son's name. There was, a few years ago, a mess up at the bank where the money exceeded what the bank would be able to hold for him. I didn't see how that came to be a problem because when I checked this morning before coming here, there was less than five hundred dollars in the bank." She asked him about offshore accounts. "I can't get to those. I could at one time, but I've been locked down for doing that."

"I'll give you access that won't be traced back to you. You've done a great job here, Mr. Caldwell. This is more than I had hoped you'd be able to find." He thanked her, his face pinking up a little. "Have you kept track of your expenses for us?"

"Yes, miss." He handed them over to her. As she was looking them over, adding them up in her head, he explained to her why some of the receipts had him taking things off it. "My wife came along with me on some of the trips. I took off the difference on the hotel for a second person. Why they charge that is beyond me. All the rooms have two beds in them anyway. The dinners too."

"Mr. Caldwell, we're sisters that are all together on everything. Do you know why? I'll tell you. We're family. Family, no matter what needs to be done, comes first every time. When you want to take your wife out with you to a nice restaurant we're footing the bill for, you do it. It'll make you feel better, and she will certainly be happy. Take her on all the work you do for us." He asked her if she'd be using him again. "Absolutely. You've done some very fine work here."

"I hate to say this, but the money has been nice. Being retired isn't what we'd thought it would be." She told him she was sorry about that. "Nothing to do with you, miss. It's just that it's too expensive to live or die. When we buried my brother last summer, it was over ten grand. I just don't think young people nowadays are cut out to be old and without." He laughed when she told him she understood that a great deal.

"Privileged, I think is what my brother-in-law calls it. Some of them, not all, think that whatever is going on that doesn't affect them, they want to part of it. I have several nieces that are being raised to work for what they want, even though their parents could well give them whatever their heart desires. I like that."

He nodded and told her about his own daughter. "Forty-two years old, and she's still living and dressing like she's just about sixteen. Acting like it, too, most of the time. No job. Nothing to show for her living in this world after she's gone. And forever with her hand out. It's why we're in the predicament we're in now. When we didn't hand it over, she'd just take it." He cried a little, and she let him gather his emotions by looking out the window to her office. "I nearly told you that she's a good girl, but she's not. Her mother and I are raising up her son like he's our own. It's her son that I feel the worst for. Knowing his mother is out there having a good time when he's stuck with an old couple that doesn't have anything left because of her shenanigans."

"I'm so sorry, Willy. I can call you that, can't I?" He knew she was older than him, so he laughed and told her that was fine by him. "I can fix some things up for you and your family."

"No, I didn't break down to have you helping me out." She told him what she had in mind. "I'm doubting you keeping this old buzzard on retainer for whatever you need would be of much help for you."

Remi nearly scolded him for saying *buzzard*. It was a name associated with her bird. Being a vulture, she had heard just about all the names people would call her if they ever found out what she'd been born as. Instead, she smiled at Willy and set him up with whatever he needed in the name of being on retainer for the birds.

After he left, she went back to her work. It wasn't hard for her to come up with some new recipes for her venture here in New Town. But the fact of the matter was, she was bored out of her mind. Everything here just seemed too perfect. There was some trouble. She knew that. Just last week, Duncan and Jude had had to put one of the people of the town in jail.

"Do you suppose I really do need a nanny to help with the kids?" Mercy was like that. Just sit down and start a conversation as if they'd been talking about whatever it was the entire time. "I'm exhausted all the time. Not just from feeding them—Joel helps with that a great deal—but taking them off the ceiling, out from under the bed. Also, and this one is scary as fuck, I have to keep an eye on them so that they don't go outside. I'm terrified they're going to simply float away."

"They're only three weeks old, Mercy. Are you telling me their magic is that powerful already?" She said it was and that they now were changing their own diapers when necessary or if she didn't get to them fast enough. "Christ, I'm never having kids. That's fucking messed up. But back to your first question. How the hell would you hire someone to watch over kids that are flying around and changing their own diapers? Just chain them to the bed and wait until they're like, in their thirties."

"It's been tempting, let me tell you. But then I look at their faces light up when they see me. That's the plan, I think. That you can't harm them while they're little and driving you to fucking homicide because they're so adorable." Mercy handed her phone to Remi. "See what I mean?"

The girls were on the ceiling of their bedroom, laughing. Joey, named for his dad, was lying on his back looking up at Beth and Sandra as he laughed too. The three of them would have had her running for cover. It made her feel good that she could have one to three babies. They were a lot of work, but she couldn't love them any more.

"I don't have anything, though, other than I'm glad I'm not you." Handing her back the phone, she could see that Mercy was really destressed about this. "Look, most everyone around here knows what we are. Why not see if you can put the word out that you're looking for a nanny for three rambunctious kids? Mary could probably help you with that. She knows everyone around here better than we do."

"I'll do that. I should have gone to her first."

She looked at the stuff she was working on when Remi offered it to her. "I don't know how many people would go for caviar around here, but I do like the other things you have here. I also love the fact that you have a listing under each item for smaller portions without calling it a kid's meal. Do you suppose you'd have prizes for them when they eat all their food? Like, they don't get it until they've eaten everything. Or at least until their parents are satisfied."

"That sounds good in theory, but I doubt it would work. I think it would piss people off more if we did that, for the simple reason that we're putting pressure on their children." Mercy said she'd not thought of that. "Normally, I'd not either, but I've been in this setting before where there was an ice cream or something for all the kids that cleaned their plates. It didn't matter to some of the parents if they ate or not, so long as they didn't whine too much and that they didn't bother them. Christ, I dislike parents that let their kids run wild in a restaurant like it's home, and they don't give a shit."

"I suppose you think you're going to have some perfect children?" It was a fair enough question, Remi supposed, but she still didn't like it. She was glad when Mercy changed the subject. "I'm going to need a new project soon. Something I can work on from home. If you have anything on the fae project, I'd like to work on it."

After answering a few questions that Mercy had, she was alone once again. Taking off the caviar, she worked on some of the other dishes she'd like to have. Remi was liking the overall menu she was creating. Having at one time worked on computers, and having Miley, Mercy's other child, helping made it easier too since she was able to work a computer almost as well as Remi could.

It was well after five when she went home. The house hunting wasn't getting her anywhere, and she wasn't happy living with Duncan and Jude. Not that they'd been mean to her or anything, but it wasn't her place. Not her things. In addition to the restaurant, Remi wanted to get herself an office front. She was going to do some design work again on logos and such.

Walking back to the castle from the new restaurant building, she thought about what she might name the place. She'd had a couple of ideas but had tossed them out as silly. She did want something that would make her stand out.

As there wasn't much competition in New Town for her to try and drum up business, she thought if she just named it *Come and Get It* that no one would care.

Everywhere she looked, people were putting things out for spring. It was still cold out, enough of a cold spike in the air to make a person shiver. But she could see signs of spring right around the corner. She paused in front of the house that Esme was having built.

It was a beautiful structure. Remi could see it finished in her mind. There were five bedrooms on the topmost floor and three more on the second level that included a master suite. She had wanted it small, one bedroom and the rest of the house, including the bathroom, all open. Personally, Remi thought Esme was doing that to piss off Mercy. But she had relented when she had it pointed out to her that she'd need more room simply to be able to paint. Esme was a very famous painter.

"Mistress? Do you have a moment?" She told Patch, the faerie in charge of the greenhouse in town, that she had lots of time. "Oh, good. You see, I was working with the others, and I swear to you I only stepped away for a few moments. But you know how our kind work. Busy, busy,

busy." She asked him to get to the point, please. "Yes. I only stepped away for a moment. When I returned, the others had planted thrice the amount of herbs you'd asked for. So instead of having just ten plants of basil, we have thirty. You can see my worry, can you not?"

"I do. Is it only herbs, Patch?" He nodded. "That's all right then. When I have my home finished up, when I find someplace, I'll want them in my yard too. I was thinking that instead of wholly flowers, I'd mix in a few herbs with them for the powerful smell they give." He said it sounded heavenly. "Thank you. So you go ahead and take care of the extra, and when I get me a house, they'll be good for me to use. In the meantime, I'll pick out a place for them to be around the restaurant too. That'll be a win-win for me."

She made her way to the castle just as Duncan was pulling into the driveway. He was a very nice man and kind to all his people. Remi couldn't have been happier with the man if she'd picked him out on her own to be king.

~*~

Rose couldn't read, so why she was looking at the magazine when she was in the doctor's office was beyond her. Putting it down with a huff, she looked around the waiting room. She hated waiting more than she did having to find something to eat that was fun and delightful for herself.

"Mrs. Herb? The doctor is ready to see you." She nodded and gathered up her things to entertain herself with. Even though she'd been told that he would see her now, she also knew it would be at least another hour or so before he would actually see her. "If you'll tell me what's brought you in today, I can get the doctor prepared to speak to you."

"I'm having some issues with being able to rest properly. Also, I have trouble concentrating. On anything." The nurse asked if she was depressed. Laughing, she answered her. "No, never that. I have everything I've ever wanted right at my fingertips."

That reminded her that she needed to contact the bank about the message left to her and Juniper this morning. They had told her she had overdrawn her checking account. That wasn't possible. They had more money than she could count most of the time. Not that she could have, but there had to be something wrong.

The nurse took her vitals, and then she was weighed. Rose was confused as to why she was suddenly putting on some extra pounds. That hadn't ever happened to her before. She'd also noticed that Juniper was graying more too. Thinking about that, she missed not only the doctor's knock to come see her but also his greeting.

"I'm sorry. I was thinking about something that had occurred to me this morning." Dr. Williamson told her it was fine, then looked at her chart. Rose did wonder if he'd be able to tell anyone what she was wearing if asked, for as much effort he'd put into making eye contact with her.

"Thinking hard on something that deeply could be why you're not sleeping, Mrs. Herb." She told him she'd not thought of it until just now. "I'm sorry. I can give you a little something to relax you enough to get to sleep. However, I'd like for you to try and keep track of what little things you think of during the day. That way, you can compare things to your thoughts at bedtime. It might just be something small, like if you'd paid your water bill or something. Little things can add up to something larger in the dark."

Taking the prescription, deciding he didn't know what the hell he was talking about, Rose decided to go to the bank while in town rather than walking home and coming back later. She hated to be carted around everywhere, but with money, one had to make a showing of it. Or at least that's what Juniper was forever telling her. It made her smile when she thought of the fun they'd had just a week ago.

They'd only just gotten back from her home she had shared with Basil. Not that he'd seen her or his brother, but she had had a good time sorting through the things in the vault, or safe as it was called around here, and taking the most beautiful things she could lay her hands on. With the exception of a few things she'd been wearing out of the thing, she had only taken things she wanted. Juniper had pulled out bag after bag of coins and gems that they'd made love on. The gems had been a painful thing to have sex on, but it was also exciting. Basil had never excited her like his brother did.

"Or how he used to." She'd been thinking of Juniper a great deal of late. He was getting heavier too. "A fat immortal is something I don't need right now."

Talking to herself wasn't something she usually did. However, Sorrel and Juniper were out scouting for a new home for them. The one they lived in now was nearly trashed. They'd done it, of course, but since they never paid for housing or the things that were in it, they didn't care how they treated their homes. The couple that had lived in the house they were enjoying were still frozen in the deep freeze in the basement. Freezers had been a life saver in not having to dig graves, she thought. Just pop them in the freezer, and they were out of sight and out of her mind.

Rose moved up one step when the three people ahead of her did. Waiting in line for anything was another pet peeve of hers. Not that she thought she was better than anyone else — she knew she was. But it never ceased to annoy her how there weren't enough people working so you could get in and out of anywhere without having a que you had to wait in.

Finally, it was her turn to talk to the teller. "I'm checking on my account." After telling the woman all the information she asked for, including shit she didn't think she really needed, the woman asked her to hold on. The clicking noises her nails were making irritated her. Everything seemed to irritate her of late. When the woman said she'd be right back, Rose was left standing at the now empty teller booth.

The bank manager asked for her to follow him. She was in his office with the door closed before she could think that perhaps Juniper or even Sorrel should be with her. Looking around for some sort of exit that would get her out of there quickly, the bank manager began to speak.

"Ms. Herb, my name is Carder Pillow. I can wait to explain this to you if you'd like to wait on your husband or son."

She nodded and pulled out her cell phone. When the stupid thing started ringing in her ear, she realized he knew she was married with a son. Juniper answered just as she was getting ready to ask the man how he knew all that.

"Can I call you back, honey? I'm having some issues with the credit card company." She said she was in the bank now and was wondering if the issues could be related. "I don't know. I suppose I'll have to make a trip in there to get this cleared up. In the meantime, don't say a word until I get there. There isn't any reason for whatever is going on. We're pillars of the community."

Perhaps he was, but she certainly wasn't.

She didn't socialize much—rarely, as a matter of fact. Rose just didn't like people—the way they spoke, the way they walked, the way they ate a meal, sloppy and talking with their mouth full. She'd been the queen of a castle at one time when there were barbarians around. Rose still ate like a queen. There was never a time when she even put a small bite in there that she spoke around it. Christ, they were all cows.

She realized that Mr. Pillow was speaking.

"How is your son?" She told him he was fine. "He was in here just this morning. That was before we got a call. The call is what I'm going to explain to you and your husband. I didn't discuss anything with your boy. I'll tell you that right now, but then, I didn't have the information I have now."

He was talking in riddles, confusing her with information she didn't understand. Rose stood up to go into the lobby and wait for Juniper when he showed up too. Sitting down beside him, she noticed something she'd not seen before. His hands had old people marks on them. The brown and black bruises were there, as well as the dark colorations of age. She'd been a nurse once, for about a week, before she realized how very important it was to know how to read. But the people she'd been caring for in that few days had explained to her they were the marks of age. Now Juniper had them.

"Mr. and Mrs. Herb, I received a call not ten minutes after your son left this establishment to inform me that your accounts were to be ceased." Juniper asked what that meant. "That we're to put a lockdown on all your spending, as well as any credit cards you might have with the bank here. I've contacted the company attorney, and he said he'd take care that all the merchants you might deal with would also be informed. I do believe they have some sort of contact with the Federal Bureau that can make that happen. I'm afraid all you have for the moment is what you might have on you in cash."

"How am I supposed to live without money, I ask you?" Rose thought it was a good question, but Mr. Pillow only said he didn't know, but the bank would be closed to them. "I'll just take it out of the ATM."

"That won't work either, I'm afraid. You see, it's a part of the bank, and that will also be cut off from you. There is nothing I can do about it, I'm afraid. My hands are tied when it comes to the way the government does things." Juniper looked at her, then back at Pillow when he spoke again. "I have no information I can share with you. Not because I was told not to share, but I simply wasn't given any hint as to what might be going on."

"Are you reading my mind?" Pillow nodded and grinned at him, his fangs showing now that he'd been ousted. "What are you doing to us? I can't believe the government would want to come down on our heads. We have done nothing."

"As I have said to you and your wife twice now, I don't know anything about what is going on. Even though there has been a large amount of money taken out of your accounts, all of them, I can honestly tell you that I don't know who did it or where it went. Again, this happened just after your son left here with about five thousand dollars. He did tell me he'd be back later for more. You see, it's not possible for us to give out more than that amount more than twice a day." Juniper asked what he was doing with the money. "I have no idea. I didn't have any reason to look into his mind at that time. Now with you, with the lack of information I got from the bureau, I took a look. You've been stealing money for a long time now, haven't you?"

Juniper grabbed her hand, and they left the office. The vampire was laughing loudly as they raced out the door and into the street. Stolen money. That's all her mind could center on for the moment. If he knew the money was stolen, he would know who they were stealing it from.

Once they were on their street to go home, Juniper finally slowed his pace. She was glad for it. Her legs, much smaller than his, were doing twice as much work to keep up.

"We have to find Sorrel before he spends all that money. It's going to get us out of here." She told him she didn't know where he was. "I'll call his cell phone. Christ, do you think Basil has finally figured it out? I wish to god we'd killed him long ago. Now this entire thing might come back and bite us in the ass."

They were walking up the walkway, her favorite part of the house, when they saw someone they didn't know sitting on the front porch. Whoever it was, they were rocking in one of their chairs and drinking a tall glass of what looked like iced tea. Suddenly Rose was quite thirsty.

"Hello. Might I help you?" Juniper pushed her behind him when the woman, she could see now, stood up. "We've only just gotten home, but if you were to allow us to go inside for a few minutes, we'd be able to talk to you. It's been a terrible morning thus far."

"You're all sweet and sugar when it suits you, aren't you? As for you getting into the house, go on ahead. I do think you'll enjoy the recent updates I've added to it. Or not. I don't care one way or the other, but there you have it." The woman grinned at him. "Your son, Sorrel. I'm assuming you are aware that he's taken out all the money you're ever going to get from the bank, correct? You'll also find that none of your credit cards will work. Other things too, but I think you figuring them out on your own will be a great source of entertainment for me and the others."

"Do you know why the bank isn't allowing us to have the money we worked hard for?" The woman said she should know two things but didn't explain them. "Why are you talking to us anyway if you've no plans to—?"

"I could explain them to you at length, but I don't want to. I have better things to do than sit around here with a couple of morons that thought stealing millions of dollars wasn't going to catch up to them." Rose asked the woman who had lied about them. "No lies, I promise you, but I am glad I got to see your faces when things started to fall apart. If you need a name to curse, I'm Remi. That's all you need to know for now."

"You're one of the queen's birds." It wasn't a question, but the woman affirmed what Juniper had said. "Why would you be here when the queen has been dead for longer than anyone in this town has been alive?"

"You fucked up."

The woman shifted from herself into a vulture. Then as she stepped off the porch to the sidewalk, she grew to a monstrous size. Screaming, Rose fell back and hit her head. They knew, was all she could think about as she passed out.

Chapter 2

Harlin Tayler tried to keep his nerves under control. This thing was about to end, and he couldn't be happier. Four years of this man was more than he ever thought this would take. His bosses and their bosses didn't think that Sorrel was nearly as smart as he apparently was. The man so far had eluded every kind of trap they'd set up for him before Harlin had come on the scene.

Being an undercover agent for the Feds wasn't what he'd wanted as part of his long-term goals. Being an agent at all hadn't been in his mind. But here he was, not only an agent but with skill sets that made it so he could go deep undercover and no one would ever know who he was. He supposed it was because of the little extra he'd gotten one night when he'd been out too late and was just a little tipsy.

Glancing at his watch again, he wondered where the hell Sorrel was. He said to meet him here at the diner at noon, and it was now coming up on twelve-thirty. Harlin decided he was only going to give him ten more minutes, and he was going to leave. Fuck this shit.

The Feds knew that Sorrel was the head honcho in some of the major drug rings. There had been so many leads going back to him that Harlin was surprised he'd not been arrested. But, as he'd found when he'd started making his way into the cartel, Sorrel seemed to be one step ahead of every bust they'd made, even when Harlin knew the man had been in the building when the Feds arrived.

That was when Harlin figured out that Sorrel wasn't just not a human, but he was fae. Sorrel had a very special way of blending into whatever their surroundings were. Or to simply change himself into whatever piece of furniture or other items that were close at hand so he could go undetected until it was safe again. Harlin could and did see him each time the place he was in had been raided. It was that skill set, the Feds called it, that made him a perfect candidate to find Sorrel and have him put into prison. And today was going to be the last time, he hoped, that he'd have to hang out with the monster.

Sorrel was a sadist. He didn't just abuse and end up killing the women he would take to his lair, what he called his playroom. But he would maim and then kill people working for him, making them suffer beyond what their crime, as he saw it, warranted. Harlin had been witness to just one of such killings, and he vowed never again. He was sick beyond anything Harlin had ever seen.

The slap to his back had him reaching for his gun. When Sorrel sat down next to him, Harlin asked for his bill. Sorrel asked him if he'd been there long.

"Long enough. I have shit to do today, so I'm going to have to meet up with you a little later." Harlin stood up, well past being pissed enough that he wanted to just kill the man, but he was sick of this job. "See you later."

"No. Sit down." He just stood there watching Sorrel. "Please? I'd like to talk to you. There is something going on at my house, and I might need you to help me with it. My parents are in trouble."

"What did they do now?" He'd heard all the stories about his parents. Not just from Sorrel, but the fae he knew, as well as the Feds he worked for. It seemed that not only had they had faked their own deaths, but Sorrel's mother was supposed to have been married to the fae king. Not that Harlin didn't believe the last part — he'd seen her with the other man — but Sorrel wasn't the king's child. "I have shit to do today, as I told you when you asked me to meet you here, Sorrel. I also explained to you that I hate having to wait on you. You either show up when you're supposed to or — "

Harlin felt the magic tighten around his body. His throat started to close up even as he stood there. Not struggling with the magic, which he could have vanquished immediately, he stared at the other man as his lack of breathing started to make his eyes water. Then it was gone.

"Christ, you're a hard ass. Sit down, please, and I'll explain to you what I need. By the way, you're going to have to teach me how to just stand there and not give a shit if you die or not. That's a wonderful trick." Harlin told him he didn't care if he died or not. "So you've told me. But I know better. Anyway, this woman showed up at my parents' house. They were told that they're in trouble. Before you ask me how I knew about this, I was hiding in the bushes beside the door when not only did the woman just appear there, but she also turned into a fucking huge buzzard."

Everything in him seemed to cease working. His mind wouldn't work, so his breathing and his heartbeat seemed to pause too. The queen's birds. Harlin knew enough about them to know they were real and that they were dangerous as fuck too. It wasn't until the pain on his face that he realized he'd blanked out for a few moments. Harlin sat down hard on the seat he'd been in before.

"I take it you know who this woman might be? Dad was going on about some kind of birds of prey that belonged to some queen when he was living around that area. I didn't really believe him until today. Christ, it was fucking huge, Harlin." He asked if he knew her name. "She said it was Demi or something like that. I was just too shocked to remember it after she just up and changed like she did. Do you know her?"

"I've heard of her and the others. But no, I don't know them. There are supposed to be six of them, all birds of prey. Larger than life." Sorrel told him that's what his father had said too. "To be honest with you, Sorrel, if these people are after you, I'd just turn myself into them. They're not to be fucked with."

"I'm not going to do that. Let my parents deal with them. They're forever afraid of shit that has nothing to do with me." Sorrel laughed. "They're going to be in for a big surprise when they find out about the deal I have going. I've done it all in their names."

Harlin nodded when he thought it was appropriate and grunted when Sorrel seemed to need a verbal answer. Instead of listening, he thought of his buddy Grant and how to get in touch with him. It had been years since he'd contacted the older man, but now he thought he had to. When Sorrel stood up, he did as well, not remembering a word that had been said.

"Okay, so I'll see you at dinner. We'll meet up at my house. All right?" Nodding, he thought of the deal going down tonight and wondered if he should ask about it. However, Sorrel brought it up when he was thinking of a way to work it into the conversation. "The deal we have going is going to hit at midnight at the dockside. You and I will be there, but we're not going to be getting our hands dirty with it. I'm not going to prison when life outside of it is so profitable. Get it?"

"Yes." He laughed, but he could hear the strain of it in his ears. "I'll see you later. I have some things I'm working on, but I'll be there on time. Will you be?"

"Yes. I said I'd not be late with you again. Get off my back, will you? I had a very good buzz going about this woman I had, and you're crapping on it. Just chill." He'd have to tell his boss that they'd have one more body to add to the count they already had. "I might even get me another piece before you get there. Hey, I know, we can share one. That'll be a blast."

"We'll see."

He wouldn't. Even if he had to cut his own dick off. There was no way he was going to have any kind of fun with a woman that Sorrel had cut to pieces, then fucked with whatever was close enough to do it with.

Shivering, he made his way out into the sunshine and was startled to see Grant leaning against his car. Ignoring him as best he could, Harlin saw Sorrel off before he went to get into his car. Grant got in the passenger side without saying a word to him. When he put out his hand, there were three trackers in it, and he just stared at him before Grant finally laughed and told him where he'd found them.

"They were on your car. All three of them were hidden in the same place as if whoever put them there was afraid one of them wouldn't work. I don't know. How the hell are you, buddy?" Harlin asked him how he knew he was going to talk to him later. "I've got a bit more magic than I did before. Besides that, we have someone watching over Sorrel and his family. When they started to do a check on the man with him, I saw it was you and decided to come see you. You do know he's on the list of beings that need to be killed, right?"

"I'm working with the Feds on this. I hate it, to be honest with you. But it's a good job. That little extra you gave me when we were in college has made me a good asset to them. I can see things differently than a person could. Their inner self, I guess you could call it." As he explained to his friend what it was he could do, Grant gave him directions to a place he was staying until this thing with Sorrel was finished. "Why are you involved? If you don't mind me asking."

"My wife—" Harlin nearly pulled off the road to find out if what he'd said was true. "Yes,

I'm married. She's amazing and one of the birds I told you about. Piper is a Phoenix. She's the most beautiful creature you've ever seen, Harlin. I can't wait for you to meet her. I'm here with one of her sisters."

"The vulture." He asked him how he knew that. "Sorrel was hiding in the bushes at his parents' home when she showed up and showed herself. I guess it scared his mother so badly that she fainted. How much do you know about Sorrel and his family?"

"He's not someone to fuck with if you're not at least able to heal yourself. How long have you been on this case?" He told him. "Then you're probably going to be able to help us with what we need more than anyone. Right now, we're not interested in Sorrel. However, after I tell the others, they might well be. But the parents we have a lot on. They nearly killed the king of my kind with iron."

"Iron kills you over a period of time, right?" He told him it did. They pulled up in front of a very nondescript home that looked too small for the two of them to turn around in if they were inside together. "I'm assuming that looks aren't exactly how they appear."

Grant was still laughing as he made his way to the front door. When he opened it, standing aside for him to join him, Harlin got out of the car. This was going to be epic. Grant had the smallest apartment on campus. Yet as soon as he let you cross over the threshold with a simple word, you could see that he was living in luxury that Harlin had never seen before.

When he stepped into the house, he was taken aback at the sheer size of the place. Not only was there a huge kitchen, but there was a living room that he could see in his own home — if and when he could afford to ever get one. Still, Harlin didn't think it would be nearly as lovely as this one, as this sort of look would cost money.

"This is my wife, Piper." He shook hands with the woman and could see that she was indeed one of the most beautiful women he'd ever seen. "This is my sister-in-law Remi. She's cooking us dinner. So don't be surprised if you have to — What's wrong?"

For a few moments, Harlin couldn't move. Not just his body, but his mind once again ceased up. Looking at the woman, all he could think about was she was far more beautiful than Piper was and that she had a magic about her that made him see she hated being stared at. Dragging his eyes from her was difficult, but he did it. He heard her let go of her breath when he did.

"Remi? What is it?" She said he was her mate. "Really? That's wonderful. You couldn't be getting a better guy than—"

"Grant, hush before you get yourself killed." Harlin looked at him, then at Remi. They were staring at each other as if they were looking for flaws. So far as he could see, Harlin didn't find a single thing wrong with the gorgeous woman. "Come on, big guy. Let's leave the two of them alone for a little while. I don't know what's going to happen here, but I have a feeling we don't want to be witness to it."

While he had no idea what Piper meant by that, he was glad for the time alone with Remi. When she turned her back to him to work with the stove, he moved to the other side of the table where she was working and leaned against the counter. Just far enough away that she couldn't hurt him if she was upset about this.

"I'm not. Upset, I mean." He asked her why she was reading his mind instead of talking to him. "I'm not sure of a great many things right now if you want the truth. Not that I could lie to you, but I don't."

"You're one of the queen's birds. Grant told me all about you when I was recovering in the hospital. I was there for a month, so he told me a great many stories. You're the vulture." She nodded, then asked him what had happened to him. "Grant was forever working with the community on projects like gardens and such. One afternoon I went with him to hang out. We shared a couple of classes, and that was how I knew him. Some man came with a shotgun that afternoon and started firing at whoever was in his sights. He thought his wife was there growing a garden instead of home taking care of him. Grant killed him and saved my life."

"He could have healed you fully, did he tell you that?" He told her he had but couldn't because of the press. "I understand that. So he gave a little of himself to you so that you'd not die. I guess I should thank him. I don't know what to do with you. That didn't come out right."

"I understand. I don't know what to do about you either. I have a job, one that I don't like but could be dangerous to you should someone I'm working with decide you'd be prime bait to use against me." She told him she'd be able to get out of whatever they had her in. "Good to know. Are you going to look at me at any time? I'd love to see your eyes. Your face, too, if you'd just turn this way a little."

She looked at him, and he saw tears in her eyes. Pulling her into his arms, he was glad that she came willingly. However, he didn't think either of them expected the surge of power that rolled over both of them with such force it blew out all the windows in the room they were in, as well as shattering anything else made of glass. Then Harlin simply passed out.

~*~

Piper couldn't help but giggle every time she thought of the damage done to the kitchen. Well, all of the house had been rocked, but the kitchen where they'd been had suffered the most damage. Right now, the couple was out in the yard talking. Piper would love to know what was being said between the two of them. Christ, they were epic.

"You shouldn't find this so funny. Not that I blame you, but they're just as new to this as you and I were." Piper let Grant hold her as she told him what she'd been thinking. "I would as well, but I think they need to work this out on their own. What I do find amazing is that not only did

Harlin get a mark on his arm, but his entire right side must be covered in sigils. Other than Joel, the rest of us weren't marked."

"I think that has to do with the fact that Joel wasn't human at the beginning. Even Bryson had a little magic before he met Blaze. But he was wholly human." Piper looked at the couple in the yard. "It could and more than likely does have to do with however much blood you gave him. Perhaps there is a greater purpose to him coming to this family at this time. To think that, I thought the hardest to be mated would be Remi. And there she is, holding hands with her mate and laughing. She isn't upset at all."

"No. She seems to be having fun. I didn't see her smiling nearly as much as the rest of you do. Even Esme smiles and laughs a great deal, even without a mate." She looked at her as Grant continued. "I think her hair is brighter too. Like it's no longer just silver, but it's a sharp silver that would and could cut into you."

"She's glowing." Grant asked her what she meant. "I guess it would be called falling in love, and it's making her magic shine through. I know she has a great deal of magic—a lot of it she's kept hidden. For instance, I had no idea that she could teleport herself from one point to the other until she did it today. Also, you might have noticed this as well, she can fly without being her bird. That is something none of us can do."

"I thought I'd just been thinking it had been a trick to the eyes. Do you suppose Harlin is going to be all right?" She turned and asked him what he meant. "He's working with the Feds to get Sorrel arrested. He's heinous, from what Harlin's got in his head. When he does kill, he makes the suffering worse than anyone Harlin has ever seen. I've seen worse, I hate to admit, but it was done during the war with the kings and queens. Sorrel seems to be mimicking their way of killing with more violence."

"Harlin will be an immortal now, so that will help him should it come to that. But you're right. We're going to have to talk to him about a few things that are going on." Nodding, she made her way to the office they'd put in their home so that they'd be able to work on projects while working on this for Basil.

Grant stopped her by saying her name. "I'm worried about him, to be honest with you. He's had a very difficult life up until now. I don't want him hurt anymore."

"Do you think it will come to that?" He said he was sure of it. "Then we'll have to make sure he isn't. Does he have family around that we should be aware of? Siblings or parents?"

"Just a grandmother in a nursing home. She is afflicted with dementia and no longer knows him, so he doesn't visit while working. He is afraid that if Sorrel wanted to prove something, she'd be his prime target. I'm assuming, now that I've thought of it, that Sorrel can't read his mind. While I was waiting on him at the diner, he didn't seem to have a clue what Harlin was thinking about him." Piper asked him if he wanted to send someone to the nursing home. "I don't know, but I would feel better about it should it come to Sorrel finding out. She's elderly with poor hearing and, as I said, dementia. However, you know as well as I do that matters little when it comes to protecting what is yours."

"I do know that." She sat down at the computer and started looking for someone to put in the nursing home that Mrs. Tayler, Harlin's grandmother, was in. "I know a doctor that works there that can keep an eye on her for us. He's been there for some time, so it won't be a problem for him to look in on her."

After setting that up, she reached out to the others to let them know what was going on. Duncan asked if they should all come there. She told him that she'd wait. Just in the event that too many of them would overwhelm the couple, and they needed to think about their job at hand.

The castle has been cleaned up for the two of you. Staff has been hired as well. I'll take care of anything that comes up while you're there. Also, Mom left a message for Harlin. I'm not sure what it means, but perhaps he will. Did you know he is part fae? Piper told him what Grant had done for him. *No. It's more than that. He's actually about half fae. His mom, I guess, was a fae and faerie mix. There isn't much of a difference, but it's their magic that he would notice, I guess. I've put out the word for someone to locate someone that might have knowledge of her. Or better yet, her lineage. Other than the note for him, there is little I know at the moment.*

Do you think we should tell him? Duncan said it would help if he remembered anything that might help them find out who he might be related to. *Do you think that's important? I mean, knowing his relatives? Oh, Harlin told Grant his grandmother is in a nursing home. I'm going to go there and check it out. If his mother was either fae or faerie, then she would be the one that had passed it down to Harlin, right?*

Usually, but with the things going on, I'd not say for certain. They both laughed. *All right. You go and talk to the grandmother, and I'll take care of what I can on this side. Also, you should know that Basil is getting stronger by the minute, it seems. Just yesterday, I saw him out in the yard with the faeries and helping with the crops. We're going to have a good amount of food this year for families, I'm happy to say. And the herb garden just beyond the castle is enormous. The drying shed has been busy day and night since you left.*

The others filled her in on things that were going on at home too. The gardens they were putting in for the kids that wanted to fulfill a requirement for college money were working out well. There were others that were assisting with the teachers for the end of year work as well, grading papers and such. Things were going much better than she'd thought they would be with so many projects in the works.

"I've invited Harlin to dinner, but he said he has to meet Sorrel for a pickup. The police are going to be there along with the Feds to make sure Sorrel doesn't slip away. I have a feeling, as does Harlin, that Sorrel won't show, and they'll have to start all over in trying to find the man. But in the meantime, Harlin will be arrested with the others, then somehow escape if what we think will happen does." Piper asked if Harlin knew he was an immortal now. "Yes. I guess he and Remi have been talking about all the things he will get. The fact that he won't die has taken a great deal of pressure off him. He's been paying for his grandmother's care since she got ill."

"We'll take care of that for him. I'm going to head over and see what I can get from her. Would you mind staying here to keep an eye on things for me? I'm expecting two deliveries from the printer. Hopefully, they were able to correct their mistakes and not make any more while at it. I have to tell you, Miley and Tracy have been saving me a lot of embarrassment when it comes to putting out a flyer for shows. I owe them both so much." Grant said he'd doubt they'd see it that way. "They don't. They think that because I'm their aunt, they somehow owe me. I'm going to nip that in the bud, too, when we get back."

As she flew to the nursing home, two things occurred to her. First of all, was that the nursing home was a shitty one. From her perspective, she could see that the roof was nearly caving in, and the yard looked as if it had only been half-assed mowed in a good long time. The second thing was, the people sitting out in the rain had no one with them and were soaked through. She was going to take care of that.

Calling Carder Pillow, she made arrangements to purchase the place. He was happy with her idea of taking control of it, but there seemed to be a problem with her just buying it outright. There were three leins on the place.

"It looks as if the place has traded hands four times in the last sixteen months." He asked her to hang on while he looked. "Ah, here it is. Yes, I remember this now. They change the names around about every six or seven weeks. Oh my. I just realized they're behind in their taxes. By quite a bit, Ms. Coby. Now I see the issue as well. It looks like on or a bit after the fifteenth, there is an influx of cash. I would imagine the payments are due for their residents. After the account is drained, they switch who the owner is. It looks to me as if the people that work there — as they have all listed the nursing home as their place of business — are the ones that empty the account until the next time the accounts are filled."

"So instead of taking care of the people

they're in charge of, they take the money and hang around for the next time their name comes up. How many people are there doing this?" He told her there were six. "Six of them. I don't suppose you know how many residents are there, do you?"

"Yes, I do, as a matter of fact. There are twenty-three. Just three days ago, Mr. Owens came in to get the money out of the account. I must clear something up for you — they do leave ten dollars in the account. I'm guessing that's so it isn't closed out. What a terrible thing to have happen to the people depending on them." She agreed with him. "The account isn't in anyone's name at the moment. It says here that Mr. Owens signed the paperwork for it to be transferred. He didn't leave a name that it was to go to, telling one of my managers here that he'd have to return with Mr. Shipley. I'm assuming he's next in line for the windfall."

"Can you put my name on there?" Mr. Pillow said he could if she were to show him some identification. Then he laughed when he told her she'd been in to do it just now. He more than likely had faked what he needed from her. "Thank you, Mr. Pillow. I owe you big time."

"No, Mrs. Coby, you don't owe me anything if you can get this taken care of. It's a shame it wasn't noticed before. But as I told you when I was working with Mr. Basil, I'm new to this area and the goings on." She told him if he were to get into trouble, he was to call her. "I will if it comes up. It might, but I don't think my boss will care so long as it was done with the people in mind. I think I might well call him up right now and let him know."

"What a splendid idea."

As soon as she got off the phone with the man, she made two more calls. One was to have a room set up for Mrs. Tayler once she had visited her. Things were moving along right now, and she wondered what the others would say when they found out she'd purchased a nursing home. Laughing, she thought they'd be jealous. Good. She loved it when she could outdo her family once in a while.

Chapter 3

Juniper sat on the porch and counted his fingers and toes over and over. It was that, or he was going to have to explain to his head what he'd just seen. The house was no longer something they could live in. Hell, nothing was what it had been. He looked over at Rose when she spoke. He wasn't even sure she was saying anything coherent anymore.

"It's all gone." He didn't let his mind dwell on what she said then. "It's nothing, Juniper. Nothing at all."

"Don't. Just don't remind me of it, please. I'm having a hard enough time just...well, I'm having a hard enough time." Juniper shivered.

"How the hell did she do that? I mean, how the hell would anyone do that? To us, for cripes sake."

"She said there were updates to the house. That is not an update, Juniper." She just would not shut up about the house. He begged her once again to shut up, and she just kept on talking. "There is nothing. Less than nothing. There is white. All white, like we're in a cloud. No furniture was there. No walls. I bet we could walk for miles and never touch anything. What are we supposed to do with a house that is nothing?"

"Shut. The. Fuck. Up. About. The. House is what you can do. Do you think I didn't see it when you did? I did. Did you not see me looking around when I stood right there with you? I was there, in the event you missed me. Also, now that you've done nothing but jabber on and on about it, I'm sick to my stomach, and I have a splitting headache. And you know what, Rosemary? I can't go in the house and find me something to take for it because—let me tell you this, so you understand it too—there is fucking nothing in the house. Just shut up." He leaned back on the chair he was in, so his head touched the house. Jerking away from it, he thought somehow that it might absorb him into its nothingness and spoke more calmly now. "She's one of the queen's birds. You remember those monsters. They were the ones that took down castles that Dante went after. I don't understand why they're still around when I know Dante was killed when the castle came down upon her head. Some say they did it, as they were angered by her for something."

"Why are they here, Juniper? I mean, what has happened that—? Do you suppose Basil is finally dead? That we might be able to go home, and you can be king of the fae? That has to be the reason she's around now. I don't know why she didn't just come out and tell us he was dead, but that has to be it, don't you think?" Juniper said he didn't know, but he thought for sure that he'd feel something if his own brother were dead. "Yes, I suppose you're right on that. I didn't think of that. I'd not have those feelings, for I didn't love him. Not at all. It was you I cherished for all the centuries I was with him."

He knew that to be true as well. They had been lovers well before Basil had been chosen to be her mate. She had wanted to refuse him, but Juniper thought about her being with Basil and the things they'd get for his reign. It had worked perfectly, too, until the baby had come along.

"We'll have to figure out a way to get some cash. Remi told us that Sorrel had money. We'll have to find him so we can get some cash and head back home. I have a feeling that is where we need to be right now." He turned and looked at the house. "I don't know what to do about the house. She's cursed it and the things inside of it. When I think of the things we stashed away for something like this, I want to hunt her down and kill her."

Juniper wouldn't, of course. He wasn't a fighter. Actually, he was quite lazy and didn't do anything that wasn't required of him. Even then, he wanted to have someone help him with even the simplest of tasks. No, he knew it was big talk, but he also knew that if it came down to it, he'd sell his own mother to get out of things that might cause him harm. Or even to require him to do much.

"Well, I guess we can sell off my ring. It's worth quite a bit, don't you think?" He nodded, thinking the cash they could get for it would be more than enough for them to have a nice dinner out before leaving this place. "You have that look in your eyes, Juniper. I'll take it to the pawn shop myself. That way, I can be assured that we have enough to get us back home and in style. I haven't any idea what you're thinking but don't. Whatever it is, don't do it or say it. We have enough going on without you going to the racetrack or whatever you were imagining doing with the cash."

"You're right. But I was thinking of a nice dinner. Not the tracks this time." But he would have, given the time. He loved watching the horses race around the tracks, and with his little bit of magic, he'd been able to win more than he had lost. "Besides, I'm banned from there now. They didn't know what I was doing, but they thought I was winning much too much for me to be new at the game. I don't understand that. If I can make some money, that's what they're there for, correct? Humans are so mean at times."

He wanted to go into the house once more, just to be sure it was still the same, but his fear of it taking him was very high. There were things going on right now that he didn't know much about, and that was what made him leery of going home too. But if Basil was dead, then he'd have to —

"Shouldn't one of the staff have notified us if Basil were dead? I mean, we were paying them well to continue on with the iron in his food. You'd think that—" Juniper had to stop and lean over to breathe. "She's killed them all. Killed the others in the house and healed my brother. Holy shit, Rose, we're in deep shit if that's what has happened."

"Maybe going home would be a mistake." He wanted to snap at her but decided he'd like to keep his teeth in his head for now. "I don't know what to do, Juniper. If we stay, we've nothing to fall back on. If we go and Basil is still alive—nay, even healed—we're going to face a lot of time in prison. You and I both know he has to know we're alive. I wonder too if he knows about—that's it. I'll appeal to his better nature and tell him I hid away our son, his and mine, so it would be safe when he started getting ill. Do you think that will work in my—I mean our favor?"

"I wondered how I was going to fit into your little plan. What do you think he's going to say when Sorrel calls me Dad? Or what am I supposed to say to him when he asks me why I was here with you all this time? That is not a good plan, Rose." There were bits of it that he could use to his advantage, but he wasn't going to tell her that. If he could get to his brother before Rose, he might be able to convince him that it was all her idea. That he was led around by his nose rather than his dick. "We have to come up with a plan to make sure we're neither one brought to justice. I have a feeling he'd have one of the birds kill us if it came to that. And that is not a way I'd like to be ended."

She was staring at him again. Rose had been doing that a great deal lately, and it got on his nerves. Everything seemed to get on his nerves of late, but the way she looked at him as if she were looking for a place to stab him made his temper flare-up. He asked her, as calmly as he could, what she was looking at.

"You're aging. I am as well, but I've been seeing it on you more and more. We're graying too as if we're losing some of our magic." He didn't have a mirror, but he could look at her. There were wrinkles where they'd not been before. Small spots on her skin like he'd seen on old humans. "What do you suppose that means? And before you say it's the queen's birds, I think I was noticing it before she came here."

They continued to walk to find their son when he thought of something else. "I fell the other day. And I have to admit, it did hurt a great deal more than I thought it should have. Also, believe it or not, I got a mark on my leg from it.

Bruise. I've never had one of those in my entire life. Now I have two of them from the bump that I took when that bird changed and scared us both." He waited for her to tell him she'd not been scared, but she wisely said nothing. He decided to come clean. "I've been a bit harsher lately as well. Like my temper is just on the edge all the time. I'm sure you've noticed it as well."

"I have. But I've had the same sort of emotional upset. I want to sob all the time now. Not just about the things you say to me, but every little thing. The other day I saw a faded rose. You know how much I love those flowers, and I cried for an hour. What is wrong with us? Why is this happening?" He said he didn't know but was glad to know she'd been having the same issues. "That wasn't nice, Juniper. However, I do understand what you're saying. What do you suppose it is? Something to do with Basil? I think you should contact the people at the castle. Perhaps they have some information we can rely on. I don't trust that woman to be telling us the truth."

"I don't either, but she seemed to know about things we didn't. I just hope Sorrel hasn't blown all the money. We're going to need that if we're going to go and see what's happening to

Remington 97

us." He had a feeling they both knew what it was. So long as Basil was dying, they were getting his magic. If he was alive and well, they would be depleted, a little at a time at first, until they were nothing more than dust. It was, he'd heard, a very painful death. Every deed done to one's body came to pass as they died. "There he is now."

Sorrel was talking to a young man. He didn't know him but didn't care. It was good that they didn't have to run him down to find him. As soon as he saw them, he turned his back to them. This wasn't a good sign. Sorrel had been acting strangely too. Not just mean, but savagely so. When the man disappeared, simply vanished, they hurried across the street to talk to their son.

"Don't you see that I'm busy? I'm trying to cut some deals here, and the two of you hanging around me isn't helping." Rose explained to him what was going on. He was glad she'd left out the part about the house. Juniper didn't think he'd believe them. "So? What does you having been locked out of the accounts have to do with me? I have money. I guess you're going to have to find yourself a job or something. Isn't that what you've been telling me for decades? It doesn't feel good to be without, now does it?"

"Sorrel, you will hand that money over right now, or so help me I'm going to—" He didn't know a single threat to hold over the boy. He supposed he was a man now, and it bothered him on so many levels that at some point, his son had gotten bigger than him. "Sorrel, we're going home. The king might well be dead, and we'll be able to live in a castle again."

"What do I need with a castle when I have everything I want right here?" Rose pleaded with him to hand over the money. "No. I'm not going to do that. What is it you're forever telling me when I have trouble? Oh yes. You've made your bed, now you must make it. I've found out too that you've been saying that wrong. It's you've made your bed, now you must lie in it. I have to tell you, it pleases me to no end that I can make you—"

"You're aging too." Sorrel put his hand over the marks on his hands. Juniper hadn't seen that until then. It was his hair—it was turning gray even as he watched him. "All of us are aging, and it won't be long until we're nothing but old people before we turn to nothingness. This is why we need to get back home. To see what is going on, so we don't end up like a human does when they've reached the end of their life cycle. Don't you see? It's our magic, our birthright, that is being taken from us."

Sorrel walked to a window and looked at himself. Juniper looked at his hands. They were worse than they'd been just an hour ago. Now they were nearly all dark brown with spots. Rose too. Her hair was nearly as white as the snow in the winter here in these parts. Whatever was going on, it was happening faster and faster now.

"Are you doing this to me? To prove some sort of point?" Rose told Sorrel she wasn't doing anything but that it was happening to the three of them. "Christ, this is just what I need. My partner is missing, I'm hurting more and more daily, and this fucking shit with my hair is for the birds. When can we get there and kill whoever is doing this to us? The sooner, the better. I have two deals going down, and I don't want to miss the action when it does."

"We'll need the money to buy plane tickets. After that, we'll have to figure out a way to get out to New Town before this gets any worse." Sorrel nodded, but he didn't look any too happy about this. "Son, we can't waste any time on this. We have to get there before it's too late. Something is going on, and we're going to die if we don't get it figured out."

"All right. But I'm pissed. Whoever is responsible for this is going to be hurting more than I am. And I do hurt. All the fucking time now." Rose and he both told their son they did as well. "If you figure out who is doing this, I want to know. I'm going to make them suffer. I've gotten very good at making people suffer."

Neither of them said anything as they made their way to the car. They realized, too late, that using magic for anything would drain them more. The moment that Rose "spruced" up her hair, making it look darker, she aged about ten more years. This was getting out of hand, and he, like his son, wanted someone to pay. He only hoped they could make it there before it was too late for them to figure things out.

~*~

Harlin hadn't been to see his grandmother in years. She'd been so out of touch with things it broke his heart that she didn't know him. Grandma Taylor didn't look any different than she had when he'd seen her. The only thing different was her room.

"We've put her in this nursing home so she'd

be able to get the care she needed. The other place is going to be shut down in a few days so it can be assessed as to whether or not it is worth fixing up. Right now, I'm thinking it's not." Remi sat down beside him as his grandma puttered around the room. He kept an eye on her as she mumbled to herself about windows and dresses.

"Mercy said she might be able to understand us." Remi looked at his grandma, then at him, winking at him. "I don't know how that is possible since she's been lost for so long. She didn't even know me."

"She knows you. Don't you, Alma?" Grandma turned and looked at Remi when she spoke. "I remember you. You were one of the daughters of Donald, the mule man. You were put into the wrong home when you were first at New Town, but your father thought the six of you could stay in a one-bedroom home so as not to be a bother to the queen. How are your sisters?" Grandma sat down and stared at them both. "You're not his grandma either, are you? But his mother. Isn't that right?"

"He was safer not being my child. And for me to be in here. Why now? I've not bothered anyone." Harlin stared at his grandmother as she continued speaking. "How are you, Harlin? It's been a while. I'm not upset that you stopped coming. It was, as I said, safer for you not to be around me. Those people would have found us out."

"What people? I don't understand what's going on. Grandma?" She told him it would be all right. "No, it's not going to be all right. Why did you lie to me? What people are you talking about coming for us?"

"Basil's wife and his brother. Their son too. I believe his name was Sorrel." Remi said that was it. "She's a monster, but that boy of hers is worse than anything that has ever been born if you ask me. You asked me why? Well, I came here to raise you after your father died. He wasn't a great man, but he was good to us. Almost as soon as I got here with you, Juniper nearly tackled me at the airport. He tried to kill me and you. If he had succeeded, he would have been able to suck all our magic from us. So I had to hide us. This was why I came up with me being insane and you being out on your own, without the knowledge that you would have had about the two of us."

"You took my memories." She said it was necessary for her to keep him alive. "I understand that, but…I'm working with him now. We're partners in this deal that…you're my mother."

"I am." She changed then. Her face smoothed out. Her hair darkened to look as fresh and new as his own. "I can return those to you now if you wish. I have been, in my own way, keeping up with the others. They're in trouble." She looked at Remi. "You've done that, haven't you?"

"My family and I have. Yes. We're the queen's birds. I'm the vulture." Grandma — or he supposed he should call her Mom — said she'd figured that out. "Also, Harlin is my mate. We're a couple now."

She was surprised by that but in a very happy way. After hugging them both several times, she held him at arm's length as she looked into his eyes. Mom had tears in her eyes as she watched him, and he brushed one of them away when it fell over her smooth, warm cheek.

"I love you so much, Harlin. Your father, he would have been so very proud of you. He was killed by Juniper. He and Rosemary, they were fooling around one afternoon, and he caught them. As he was on his way to tell the king, they cornered him and did unspeakable things to him. Then they tossed his broken body on my doorstep and said I'd better be watching myself." He told her he was sorry for that. "That wasn't the end of it. Several days later, as I was hanging out the wash, I had you in a small crib. You were enjoying the sunshine. When I turned, I saw that Juniper had you in his arms with a knife at your throat. I was terrified that he was going to kill you. The next day, I left home and came here. After that, I made it so you had no memories of this place or your life from New Town that someone could use against you. It was the hardest decision I've ever made, but one I'd do over again to keep you as safe as I could."

"There are a few things I need to tell you, Alma. One of them is that the two of you are immortal. More so than you were before. Nothing can kill you. The removal of your head would be impossible, and nothing can penetrate your heart. The reason I'm telling you this is that we're about to have company, in the form of Sorrel. Just do as I say. Oh, the second thing is, you're both able to shift into a bird and fly away." Remi went to the window and opened it up. "I'm sure of that since you're part fae, correct?"

"Yes. Both of us are." Remi told them they needed to get out of there now. "I don't know if I can fly again."

"Fake it then. Get out of here while I deal with this fucker." He went to the window and watched his mom as she shifted to a beautiful fae creature he'd never seen before. "Give him his memories, Alma. I'm assuming the memory of flying will be there for him."

Mom touched her hand over his heart, and he felt like she'd hit him there. But almost as soon as the pain touched him, it was gone. All his memories of his father and mother were brought back to him in a single moment. Remi said once again they had to leave.

"I can't. Not without you." She asked him if he knew how to use his newfound magic. "No. I guess not. But you will be careful."

"I will. Now go. I can't kill this fucker while worrying about you." He felt the shift take him and didn't have time to look at himself as he was literally tossed from the window, laughing when the wind picked him up, and he soared over the skies. It was the explosion of something entering his mom's room that had him turning back.

Don't, Harlin. She was correct in sending you away. Come. We'll go to the trees and find shelter there. He didn't want to. His mate was there and could be hurt. *She can't die, Harlin. And if you're there, she will get harmed trying to protect you. Remi has been a warrior since long before you were born and will be the only thing that comes between you and being hurt forever. We'll hide. Then when she's dealt with the issues, we'll meet up with her again.*

They landed in the trees not far from the nursing home. He couldn't see what was going on and thought that was better. If he could see her getting hurt or even in trouble, he wasn't sure he'd be able to stay away. His mother spoke to him as they waited for Remi to come back to him.

Your father was fae. A powerful man in his own right. When we wed, there was much celebration. Basil was ill even then, but he was still a hardy man. Rosemary, his wife, wasn't a nice person, not when compared to the man he was. However, he was doing a good job of keeping the fae out of harm's way. When Rosemary got pregnant, the man was besotted to the point of being sappy about the prospects of a child. Harlin asked her how he'd found out the child wasn't his. *He didn't know, not then. I'm supposing he knows now. But it was said that his wife died in labor, taking the newborn child with her in death. Then the rumor surfaced that she'd killed Juniper for some misdeed he'd done to her. I never knew what that was.*

But no more than three days later, I saw the two of them with a newborn child. I knew it was a dangerous thing to try and approach their kind about it. The household, too, was in on things going on. They were loyal to only Rose and kept the secret from him. I do believe they might have had a hand in his near demise as well.

Iron. He was being given the iron that was in his body when the birds went to see him. Mom nodded, and he looked at the nursing home window again. The screams being heard were not that of a female. *She saved us and the king. I don't know who took the iron from his body, but it had to be one of the birds to have done it. Remi told me it was the size of a ball, so much had been given to him. I wonder what will happen now.*

Just then, he saw people racing from the nursing home. Then the fire alarm was sounding. As the people below them raced as far as they could away from the building, Harlin saw the middle of the building burning. Just then, an explosion blasted, hard enough to rock the tree they were in, and he saw Remi flying from the window and past them as the place burned hotter, engulfing the entire building.

He was ready to go after Remi when she landed in the tree beside him. She was her vulture, larger than he was as his fae, but she didn't look harmed. When she asked him if he was all right, Harlin nodded, then asked her if she was as well.

This is going to be trouble. Not for me, but for Basil. We'll have to go back home today and let him know that the man who was supposed to have been his son is no more. Mom asked her how she'd killed Sorrel. *I took out his heart. Then I removed his head. He vanished in seconds, so there will be no trace of him being there. However, with the cameras in the place and them seeing him enter with his weapons out, he will be thought to have caused the fire and was killed in it.* Harlin asked her again if she was all right. *I am. I swear it. I wish I'd had time to make him suffer as he had so many before, but with the fire rolling through the building and the people needing to get out, I thought taking my time would have cost more lives than not.* Mom thanked her. *We're going to have to go now. I'm sorry, but we'd better get ahead of Juniper and Rose before they make it home.*

Do you know why Sorrel came here? Did he know what I was or anything like that? Remi told him that he knew his mother was here, and he knew in some way that she was involved in him not being able to get any money. *He would have tried to kill her.*

*No, he **would** have killed her. He was the son of the queen of fae, no matter who fathered him. Until Basil disowns her or kills her — what I'd do if I were him — then he was the heir to the throne. Now Rose is if anything should happen to Basil. But it won't. He's been healed by one of us and is now as immortal as we are. He'll be so happy to see you two. Mercy told him that we're on our way there.* He didn't know how that worked, but Remi flew off the branch and into the sky. *We'll make good time flying like this. It will take us a while, but I'm used to flying. If you need to rest, just let me know, and we'll stop to rest. Otherwise, we should be home by morning.*

Harlin struggled for the first hour or so, not in need of a rest but getting the hang of flying again. The memory was there of him knowing how to do it, but it was only a memory and not something he'd practiced. Even taking off and landing was giving him fits until he watched his mom do it a couple of times. She confessed that she'd been flying at night when the place was closed up. He was going to have to get more practice if he was going to keep up with his mate.

I didn't want to tell your mother, but Sorrel brought other men with him when he came into the nursing home. I couldn't save all the residents but as many as I could. A few of the people were caught in the crossfire when things started to go down. He asked her if his mom had been friends with any of them. *Doubtful. She'd been keeping to herself for some time now. I'm sure she knew a great many of the residents, as well as knew what was going on at the other place. As soon as we can, we're going to have to talk about some things. Mostly what you got from me when we came together, and the things I got from you. I can feel the power you have. And when your mother gave you back your memories, I felt even more of it come to me. Your father also had some for you that you got when your mom let it go.*

I don't have anything, Remi. I mean, the very little I had when I was working went to take care of my mom. I don't know what it is you have, but it's all we have at the moment. She told him that neither of them would have to worry about money. *I worry about money all the time. It's not a pastime for me, but it is high on my lists of worries.*

We're billionaires, Harlin. More than that, we're billions of dollars times infinity wealthy. And we continue to make more money every day. What I have is now yours. What the birds have is now yours as well. The six of us, we share everything. When I make a buck, we all make that buck. The same with the others. I promise you, you are going to be just fine. And in that, so will your mother. He flew for a while, thinking on what she'd said about money. *Don't worry about it. There are more important things that we have to do first. Like finding us a home so I can fuck your brains out. That is what you should be thinking on.*

He did and nearly fell out of the sky. Her laughter, strong and happy, made him smile. Harlin did wonder about a couple of things, one of them being what he wanted in the way of a house. Now that it was planted there in his head, he wanted to have a large home where his mother could live with them, as well as a houseful of children. But only if Remi wanted them. He knew better than to put any kinds of restrictions on a woman and her body. He wasn't stupid.

Chapter 4

Rose knew her son was dead. It had nearly torn her apart when she felt the removal of his heart. She could still almost hear it beating when his head had been removed as well. Whoever had done such a thing to her only child was going to pay. She looked out the window of the airplane they were on and tried to control both her sorrow and her temper. When Juniper put his hand over hers, she wanted to jerk away, tell him to leave her alone, but she didn't.

"He knew they were around. Why he didn't stay with us, I'll never understand. There is safety in numbers. I've told him that a thousand times." Rose nodded at Juniper but bit her lip hard enough to draw blood. Starting an argument now would only cause more trouble between them. They'd been warned once already by the stewardess. She said the next time, they'd land and take them off the plane. "He was going after that woman again, wasn't he? I could only feel his death, but it was painful enough that I missed the face of the person who did it. Was it the queen's bird? The one that kept us from our home?"

"It was." She turned and looked at Juniper and slipped her hand from his, pretending to wipe her face. "He was killed quickly. I know that too, but it makes it no less painful for what happened to him. He was our only child, Juniper. I don't know what I'm to do now. He's gone."

"Yes. But we got the money from him first." Turning away again, she put her hand in her lap and wanted to draw on her magic to give herself a weapon. She wanted to kill Juniper where he sat. But making it so they had identification so they could get on the plane had cost them so much. Rose hadn't looked in the mirror yet, but she could almost feel her age taking her beauty away. "Just think, we'll be home in four hours. I bet things haven't changed a bit, don't you? I mean, I know they were working on the castle when we left. I'm sure it's no better than it was before. Who would have been on top of the workers? No one, that's who. And I'm betting that Basil is near death by now. I have tried to contact the staff we had in place, but they seemed to have been cut off from me."

"Do you think them dead?" He asked her who would have had such strength to kill them all. "I was thinking the very same bird that killed my son. She had to be powerful in order to have killed him like she did. I'm telling you right now, Juniper, I'm going to make her pay for what she's done."

With a pat on her leg, he told her that things would work out. There were so many questions going through her mind right now that she wanted to scream. How did he think things were going to go better? They were without their child. Didn't he feel that as she had? What did he think was going to happen when they arrived there? That they'd be welcomed with open arms? She'd bet anything that they'd be met at the gates to New Town, or even the fae lands, by the birds. Not that it was any of their concern what happened in their world, but the very fact that they had already stuck their feathers in where they didn't belong made her think they were a short plane ride from death. So long as she was able to extract payment for the death of her son, she'd willingly have her own head removed.

Pretending to be asleep, she thought of a dozen or more plans and tossed them out. Rose knew some things that Juniper didn't. Like the queen's birds would and could kill whoever they wanted. Even all the humans in the world if they felt like it. Even, she thought sadly, her own baby boy.

When the plane came to a jerky stop, she waited until everyone on the plane was off before she stood up. They'd had to fly coach and not what they had wanted. If it had been up to Juniper, he would have charted them a plane to go home in with just the two of them on board. It was just dawning on her how much he was worthless when it came to saving money. She'd bet anything that had she not taken the money from him when she had, they'd not have two coins to rub together. Much less enough to fly home. Rose hoped there was someone there that would end her misery and kill Juniper as soon as they landed. But it would never happen that way. She'd have to deal with him forever. It took her a long time to remember why she'd liked him at all.

Rose had begun to hate the other man. Wondering if there had ever been a time when she loved him, she stared at him while he waited on the line of people to leave so he could get their carry on. It was only an empty bag with a few magazines in it, but he had acted like it needed its own overhead compartment when they'd gotten on this morning.

It had taken her a while to figure out the money system with the humans. It wasn't like they had at home, where bartering was the way to go when a family or a person needed something. Even work was done in a way that no one would have to exchange dirty money or coins to have it done. Human money was dirty too. Nasty, as a matter of fact.

Credit cards had given her so much trouble she'd finally cut them all up and carried money around when she could. It was cumbersome, but it kept her from overspending and having to pay off a bill each month when it arrived. That was what had gotten them into deep trouble when the cards were presented to them — the realization that they'd have to be paid off. That there wasn't an endless supply of money on them that you never had to worry about. To this day, Juniper still had trouble with it. That was why she handled all the money. Or when she could, she made sure she had it before Juniper did.

Disembarking, she was hit with the smell at first. Nothing smelled cleaner than the air out here. As they were making their way up the ramp, she thought of the million and one things she needed to do yet. One of them was to contact Basil and see if he'd forgive her. She wanted out of this mess with Juniper in the worst kind of way. When her name was called with Juniper, she looked up at the man and woman standing there. While she didn't know them, the magic coming off them was so strong she was ill with it. It wasn't until he spoke that she found herself down on her knees and bowing her head.

"I'm happy to see you have retained some manners, Rosemary. You've been causing a great deal of trouble for those you left behind. I do hope you're willing to reap what you have sown." She said she was sorry. "I'm afraid that sorry does not cut it. You and Juniper are going to pay for your crimes and do so without complaint. Basil is going to join us at my estate."

"Basil?" She didn't look up to see if anyone

answered Juniper. But since he spoke again, Rose figured they had. "I last heard he was on death's bed, your lordship. I'm sorry. But I don't believe I know who you are. You have the magic of someone powerful, and I do wish to submit to you, but I don't believe we've met."

"This is my wife, Queen Judith, Wife of Duncan Neal Dante, Queen of Duncan Castle, Lady of the Realm. I am King Duncan, only son of Queen Dante, Queen of Dante Castle, Lord of the Realm." Rose did glance at them then. There was no way this was Dante's child. She never had any children. "And yet, here I stand. Rose, you would be better off thinking better thoughts than how you will kill one of my birds. I will deal with you and your husband directly. For now, you will be put in arms and taken to my castle."

Then he laughed. There was no mistaking that laughter as being from anyone but Dante's child. He brayed like a jackass, as she had done. Never a lady-like twitter, as Rose had. No, Dante would throw back her head and laugh at anything and everything that touched her fancy.

Rose's arms were suddenly in shackles. Her ankles too. Rose could walk, but it was cumbersome with the weight of them dragging between her feet. Juniper never shut up about how he was brother to the king of the fae and not subject to the laws of the king of the castle. He, too, was shackled, but his were heavier and seemed to be tripping him up more.

As for what he was talking about, Rose knew better. They all answered to this man and his wife. The other realm kings and queens were only in the area by the grace of the man that ruled the lands. It was the same with his mother and the king that died while she was married to him.

There had never been a time when they'd gone hungry or without when the queen had decided to take over the castle. Rose had wanted to hate her for what she was doing. Running around like a butcher's wife, working herself to the bone and never taking a break. But the more she saw of her and the people that served her, Rose saw that they genuinely loved her. They trusted her too to make sure they were safe when the overlord, the king of the country, had said he was going to marry her.

Not only had Dante made sure that her own people were safe from others coming to harm them, but she also made sure the fae and faerie alike were taken care of. She offered them not only shelter but wagons to move their belongings. The usage of her birds to carry whatever was too large for them to move. Not only did Basil make sure their people were taken good care of at the same time, but he'd also gifted the queen quite a few fae for them to use. It had been a good working relationship. She wondered why she was only thinking about it now.

She looked at the limo that the king and queen were getting into. At one time, she had such things to use. A car and servants. She'd had things that were hers and hers alone. Juniper and she had robbed the coffers when they needed more money. Not only that, but they'd paid the people working in the fae realm to murder Basil. Rose wondered why she'd done such a thing.

Basil had been good to her, she thought as she was put into a large van and locked to the floor with her chains. The woman with them — another bird, she didn't doubt — said nothing but made it clear that she'd not hesitate in killing them if it came to that. Rose kept her mouth shut and thought about her life with Basil.

"He's alive." She nodded at the woman — she'd not caught her name — and asked if he was all right. "Yes. My sister removed the iron from his body, and he put it on display in his home. Neither you nor anyone else will ever be able to harm him again."

"I've no wish to do that. I was only just wondering why I did it in the first place." The woman started naming off things. Greed. Stupidity. Ignorance. Cutting her off, as she was hitting too close to the very reasons, she spoke to her again. "Who are you? I'm assuming you're a bird. Which one?"

"You've met me. I'm Remi. The vulture." She nodded and looked out the small opening just to her right. "If you think to get into his heart or head again, you won't be able to do that either. You've fucked up royally, and you're going to pay the price."

"You're the one that killed my son." She nodded and smiled. "I would appreciate it if you'd not show so much happiness about it. He was my only child."

"He and his gang went into a nursing home to murder any and all residents that were there. Sorrel didn't care if someone, a child, for instance, would have been caught in the crossfire. He was there for one thing, and that was to kill my husband's mother." She didn't bother asking her if she'd deserved it or not but watched her face as she continued. "I gave him an easy way out of the punishment that he would have gotten here. And he would have been brought back here. I would have carried him in my claws and brought him. His heart was black as the stones from a fire. His blood ran so thin that I think it was as happy to escape such a monster as I was to kill him. Nay, he needed to suffer. Had I the time, I would have made it so."

"He was a man who liked diversity." All Remi did was lean over and touch her finger to her knee. The images, all of her son doing heinous acts to people—men and women alike—were so awful that she had to beg for it to stop. When it did, finally, Rose leaned over and puked. Her belly, her mind, and her heart couldn't handle such atrocities. "You lie."

"You know as well as I do that I cannot lie to you. Even though you have left your husband to fend for himself, you are still his mate until death you do part. No, that was your son, and you knew what he was like. Not only that, but you witnessed it enough when he was younger, but you turned your back to him."

"What's she talking about, Rose?" Remi did

the same to him, touched him on the knee and let him see their son. When he did the same, puked several times on the floor, Remi leaned back and smiled at them both. "That can't be right. You made all that up."

"Whatever makes you rest easy at night, you go on thinking that." The van stopped, and Rose watched the woman stand up. "You will have a trial of sorts, then you will be executed. Sadly, it will be quick and your heads removed. Once you are both dead, your bodies will be cut into pieces and dropped into the sea. Your hearts and head will be hidden away so you can never be made whole again." Juniper said she couldn't do that. "Oh, but I can. My husband and I are going to rule the fae world while Basil takes some time to himself. You have shit in my field, and I'm so very happy that I get to make you pay."

Remi got out of the van, and they were left alone. "She does that, and no one will ever be able to put us in a garden, Rose. We'll never see the rapture of our kind. Does she know that? That isn't fair. I'm going to have to talk to my brother about this. I will not allow this to happen to us. We deserve so much more than being shunned from all that we are."

Rose laughed. It was funny, really, to think that Juniper thought they deserved more than they were getting. The fact that they were being killed quickly was a blessing, she thought. After what they'd done? Well, she was hopeful it really would be quick. Rose was glad it would soon be over.

As they were hustled from the van, Rose noticed there was a line of people on either side of the road where they were headed. She knew the jail here was underground, so any creature there would not be able to see the sun. Also, there would be no warmth. The niceties that Juniper thought they deserved were gone.

Stones were thrown at them from the very people she had at one time ruled. There were blows to her head, breaking open her skin, so she bled a great deal. Juniper screamed at them to stop, to pay them the respect they deserved. All she wanted to do now was get this over with. To have her life ended now instead of later.

She had no change of heart, she supposed. Losing her son had taken a great deal from her. Rose said nothing as she was put into a cell. Sitting on the only piece of furniture in the room, a large carved stone that resembled a chair, she let her tears fall. Remi was right. She had fucked up.

~*~

They'd been playing around all day, and all Remi wanted to do was find them a nice dark place—or lighted up, she didn't care, so long as she could have Harlin take her hard and fast. She didn't need romance right now. Her body was primed, ready to take him, and everything kept getting in the way. Today she was going to jump him even if she had to take him to the highest mountain top.

He came around the corner of the table and grabbed her hand.

"Where are we going?" He turned so quickly that she stumbled against him. "Christ, Harlin, you're as hard as stone. I do hope you're finding a place for you to fuck me."

"You're such a romantic." He jerked her body to his, kissing her savagely. She nearly had him naked before she realized they were on the very mountain top she'd been thinking about. "Having a little extra magic helps in situations like this."

The burn in her body was tearing her apart. Harlin's hands were everywhere, yet they didn't seem to be anywhere for very long. As soon as he took her nipple into his mouth and suckled hard, Remi came hard enough to make the birds fly away. He dropped before her and took her pussy into his mouth before she could protest.

Remi had never enjoyed oral sex before. It was sort of anticlimactic. But whatever Harlin was doing to her body right now, she thought for sure he was going to kill her. Every time his tongue stroked a part of her, she came. When his fingers joined his tongue, she could no more stand up than she could have begged him to stop. The cool grass beneath her back was heavenly compared to the hard bark of the tree she'd been standing against.

"I'm sorry. I need you." She begged Harlin to hurry. "Christ, I'm so close to coming right now that even when I enter you, it's going to be too much."

He didn't enter her. No, that would have been too slow for the two of them. He slammed forward into her body so fully that Remi fainted from the connection they formed. When she looked up at him when she woke, his body hard and wet with sweat, she watched his wings spread out behind him, his face turn to his other self, and she knew she was with the one and true Harlin of the fae.

"Come inside of me, Harlin. Please. I need to feel you fill me." He grunted something in fae. She might well have understood it if he'd not come in that moment. "More. I need all of you."

She got what she wanted. All of him. As his cock filled her body with his juices, she felt their magic intertwine into something powerful. The climaxes took her, over and over, with such ferocity that she forgot to breathe. Her mind blanked out to the point where she couldn't remember her own name.

The climax that was building, despite her coming nearly a dozen or so times, was making her dizzy with the hunger her body was creating. When Harlin wrapped them both into his wings, wrapping around the two of them in a cocoon-like way, she cried out once more, screaming out his name in every language she knew until she simply blacked out.

When she woke up, they were still wrapped together. Touching her finger to his wing made him giggle. As he released her from the warmth, she realized that at some point, they had made it back to the room she'd been using since she'd come to the castle.

"I think we need a home. And soon." She nodded at him as his wings curled around him again. "You're going to have a child. I should have said something sooner, but when you didn't object, I couldn't have stopped myself had I wanted to."

"I remember you telling me that. But I was too…I was just too everything to remember the words." He asked her if she minded. "No."

Her body began to feel weak all of a sudden. She could hear Harlin talking to her, but she couldn't seem to form any words. Her mind was buzzing, and her heart started to beat too fast. As soon as the pain took her breath away, she screamed and screamed as blood flowed from not just her ears but her nose as well.

~*~

Harlin held her in his arms while Basil looked her over. He kept clicking his tongue at his teeth but not saying much of anything that was helpful to him. He'd cleaned up the blood before the king had arrived, but now all he wanted to do was toss the man out of the room and beg Remi for forgiveness. Pulling her tighter into his arms, he noticed the small pair of wings that were forming at her back.

"What's happening to her? She was fine until after we made love. Even then, she seemed to be all right." Basil sat down, and when the others, the birds and their mates, joined them, he knew something terrible had happened, and he'd done something irreversible to his mate. Mercy asked him how he wanted this. "Straight up. Until it gets to be too much, then shut the fuck up. What's wrong with her?"

"Remi is no longer a bird. She can shift into one, but she's not a bird any longer. She's all fae." That didn't seem to be too bad. But then he didn't have any idea what she'd think about not being one of the birds. Basil continued. "She's also carrying a child. Of that, I'm sure you're aware."

"Yes. But I don't understand what happened to change her into a fae, nor why she won't wake up." Mercy answered that. "So she's evolving? Why? I mean, I don't know anything much about what she was before. Do you think she'll be all right with being a fae with me?"

"I'd say it's a little too fucking late for that, don't you think?" He growled at Mercy when she spoke to him. "You asked. But in answer to your stupid question, I don't think she'll mind at all. So long as you're with her."

"I think this has a great deal to do with what I spoke to you about earlier. You taking over for me. The magic needed to be assured you'd have fae children, and it made sure she would have full-blooded fae children." Harlin asked Basil what that had to do with it. "The rules. There are always rules. But the rules state that a man or woman that will be ruling the fae must be a full-blooded fae. The female must be able to have fae children to take over the realm at some point, and the male must be fae to implant them into his queen. I do believe the decision for you to take over for me has been decided by the magic. I don't think anyone would be any more perfect than the two of you if you want the truth." Basil laughed.

"This is not fucking funny. What do you think she's going to do to you when she wakes up and finds out she's no longer her bird but fae? I'm not going to be able to protect you from her. And right now, I'm not sure I would. Why the hell didn't someone tell me this?" Basil told him it was in the handbook. "You mean the book that was given to me when I was about five? The one that is older than I am? Christ man, do you have any idea how long ago that was? How the hell was I supposed to remember all that stuff?"

"You're talking too loud." Harlin felt his mouth snap shut and looked at Remi, who was staring up at him. "What the hell did you do to me? I mean, I feel like I could take on a man as large as a house and come out on top."

"You're evolving into a fae." Harlin glared at Mercy. "I needed to tell her first. You'd have fucked it up by being all sweet and kind about it." Mercy looked at Remi. "Also, you're going to be the queen of the fae. And you're having a baby. Lucky you. Woo hoo."

"Is this true?" He nodded at Remi and asked her what she was thinking. "Right now, nothing much other than how good I feel. Also, slightly embarrassed that all these people are in our room right now. We need to really find us a house."

"You'll take the castle." Once again, Harlin glared at someone. Basil kept laughing. "It'll make it to your specifications. Also, there are any number of fae and faerie around that would leap at the chance to work with the new king and queen."

"Did I miss something here? When did we agree to be the king and queen of anything?" He jumped at the chance to answer her question when Blaze beat him to it. "I see. So instead of us thinking on it, we've been volunteered by magic. I suppose it could be worse. Right?"

When she moved out of his arms and stood up, he watched as wings, as large as his own, uncurled from her back and opened up. She was standing in front of the mirror looking at them when he shooed the rest of them away. It was time the two of them had a talk, without everyone there laughing and having much too much fun at their expense. She looked at him when he noticed the most beautiful crown he'd ever seen atop her head.

"You have one too. It's very ornate, don't you think?" It was, but it was beautiful. "I hope we don't have to wear these all the time. They'll get in the way of me trying to fly. I'm assuming I can fly with you?"

"Yes, I think so. I have a handbook around someplace. Mom might even have a copy of it." She told him she had it implanted in her mind. He thought of it and watched as it appeared in front of him, revealing the page of things she could do once she was fully evolved. "I don't know if you are or not, but I have to ask. Are you all right with not being a bird any longer?"

"I'm not sure, to be honest with you." She

turned in the mirror and looked at herself in the full length of it. "This is prettier than a vulture, don't you think? And I do look fantastic in this crown."

"I think you look beautiful in anything you have on. Or off." He held her in his arms. When she looked up at him, he saw things he'd not before. "Your eyes have changed. They're no longer dark but the color of the greenest grass. There are stars in them, as well as a beautiful blue. You are fae, my love."

"I love you as well, Harlin. So much." She laid her head on his chest, and he could feel the way her mind was working. He didn't pry, even though he wanted to find out what had her so preoccupied at the moment. "We need to check out the castle, I guess. As well as figure out what we're going to do with Rose and her husband."

"Basil told me last evening that he wanted nothing to do with their trial or their sentencing. He's leaving that up to Duncan. Or I guess he might leave it to us now. I don't know. I'll have to talk to him." She asked him if she should be able to feel the earth calling to her. "I don't know, love. I've never been a king of fae before. But if that's what you feel, then I'm sure it's right. I have always felt the call, but it was never like it is now. Strong enough to have me want to go and check on it. Is that what you feel?"

"It is. Like I not only need to go out and touch the grass, but I need to have a long talk with it as well." He took her hand into his and led her out onto the decking outside of their room. When he took her into his arms, and they dropped to the ground, her laughter sang all over the woods behind them. Harlin thought she could and would draw all manner of creatures to her with that alone. "I can feel it. All of it. Trees and plants alike welcoming me to their hearts."

"I can feel it as well. It's an amazing feeling."

He was enjoying being fae through her eyes. He had to speak to his mom and thought of her. When she landed in the grass beside the two of them, Remy invited her to sit with them, and they spent most of the evening and well into the night sitting and talking to whatever came out of the woods to speak to them.

Chapter 5

Basil was quite pleased with himself. Not that he would wish what had been happening to him on anyone. But he was free of the poison in his body, and not only that, his wife and brother were being brought to justice for it. Looking around at the crowd that had formed for the trial today, he could see many people he'd not seen in a very long time.

"How are you feeling, Basil?" He was standing up when his lordship Duncan told him to sit. "We're not as formal as you'd think. I'm taking cues from my mom on how to let my people be able to come to me when there is a problem. I'm to understand from Remi that you're not going to sentence your wife and brother."

"No. I think it should be left up to her and Harlin to do it. It'll show that they're not going to be tolerant of breaking the laws. Also, I think they've already done more for my people—their people—than I ever did. And they've only been king and queen for less than two days." Duncan mentioned how he'd seen them at the storage house earlier. "Yes. They were there taking an inventory. I'd not been able to do that for some time. I guess they're going to make sure it's cleaned up and out at least twice a year."

"Good for them." They watched the people for a little bit more before Duncan spoke again. "I've heard that Rosemary isn't doing well. They wonder if she is willing herself to die. The killing of her son, though I know it had to be done, has taken its toll on her. I think, should they have stayed here and not had all this other drama going on, things would have been different."

"Yes. I suppose it would have been. My wife was never faithful to me, I guess. I'm not saying I was the best person for her, but she was having an affair with my brother from the very start. Even before. I have been to speak to him. He, of course, is saying that since he is my blood brother, I should at least give him a sentence that will make it so he can live." Basil laughed a little. "I guess there are people like him, even in humans. Thinking that whatever they've done can be washed away simply because of who they're related to. Sad state if you ask me."

"Are you going to see if he can get a lesser punishment?" Basil shook his head and told him it was out of his hands. "Good for you, Basil. However, you should know that Remi is thinking, only because he is your only living relative, that you would want them to do that. Give Juniper a lesser sentence than the death that he deserves."

"I know. That's why before this begins, I'm going to dissolve my relationship with him and Rosemary. It's an old law, saying that when a sibling or other blood relative has created trouble for the pip, then the king can and should take them out of his lineage so there will be no favoritism." Duncan asked how it worked. "Nothing to it, really. I've already spoken to Harlin—now there is a smart man if you ask me, and Remi is his exact opposite in the way she is very outspoken. Anyway, I've spoken to him, and he is going to grant me time at the start so I can do this. He's all for it. Then when the trial is over, Rosemary and

Juniper have their hearts and heads removed. That is mostly ceremonial. It simply means because they'll never be whole, no one can visit them at a faerie circle and call them forth. Just to talk to them and such."

"I wish I had done that for my mother. I would love to talk to her on occasion." Basil started to tell him they'd gladly do that for him when he continued. "But she told me I've been wasting too much time talking to a dead old woman and that I should get on with my life. I think she's right in that. If I could see her like a thing a faerie ring would grant me, I'd never leave her side."

As more people started filling out the large open field, some of the other birds and their families joined them. Basil was handed an infant as soon as Mercy and her husband joined them, and he looked down at the little boy. Basil wondered if they knew the power this young one had.

"They know." He looked up at Remi when she sat down in front of him. "He's been a handful with his power. I heard Mercy telling someone the other day that she was terrified he will figure out more things to do and their house will be destroyed or something. He's a cutie, don't you think?"

"He is. I've never held a child before." She said he was a pro at it. "Thank you. Now, what is it you're here for, my dear queen? You don't usually start out with something entirely different than what you want to say. So say it so that we can talk about other things."

"Rosemary is dead. They found her body earlier this morning, and she was just skeletal remains. She also left you a note. I have it here should you want to read it." He asked her if she'd read it to him. "I can tell you what it says. I don't usually read other people's mail when it's addressed to them, but I didn't want her saying something to you that would hurt you any more than she had."

"She's asked for forgiveness." Remi nodded. "Anything else? Did she want me to have mercy on my brother? I won't do that in the event that's something she asked for."

"No, she said for you to take him to task in all, and then she listed some of the things we're going to bring up here. She also wishes you a long and happy life." He looked down at the child in his arms and let the tears flow onto his soft cheeks. "Basil, she said to tell you that you're not to worry over what happened to Sorrel. He honestly was not your child."

He burst into tears then. "I thought he might have been. You've no idea how much I wanted it to be so, right up until he was killed. Then I thought of all the things I knew about Rosemary and Juniper, and I was heartbroken to think, even for a small time, that they'd stolen away my son." Remi put her hand onto his as he held the child to his heart. "Thank you for that. Remi. You're going to be a wonderful, compassionate queen." She snorted, and he laughed. "Or perhaps we'll leave that part to Harlin."

When Juniper was brought from the cave he'd been housed in, Basil could see that his magic was fading. He'd be dead by the end of the week. Perhaps sooner. Wondering where the magic was going, he only had to look at Remi when she stood up to go to her mate to see that she was getting all of it. Then she spread out her wings when Harlin did.

"Good Mother Earth." He'd not meant to say that out loud, but now that it was out there and everyone had turned to look at him, Basil stood up and went to the couple. "You're them. The King and Queen of Forever. I never thought to see such a sight as I see before me now. You're the couple this world and many others have been waiting for forever."

"You'll have to explain that to us later, Basil." He nodded and started away when he realized that Harlin was right. "No, please stand with us. We'd both like to have your input on this as we go on."

"Yes, all right." Juniper stood up and asked where Rosemary was. "She's dead, Juniper. She let the magic go and has left this earth. She has asked that I forgive her, which I've not decided to do as yet. She also gave this couple a list of misdeeds that the two of you were up to when you were still within the boundaries of fae territory."

"I wish for you to forgive me as well, my brother. I have messed up badly, and I ask for your mercy and forgiveness. I do not wish to be put to death but to serve the time left to me by making up for what you deem as doing bad deeds." He told him it wasn't up to him. "Sure it is. You can ask them to do whatever you want. I just lost my son and my wife. The very least you can do is to consider that punishment for everything else."

"I don't have any say in what you're going to be tried for, Juniper. But I would like you to know that I am no longer your brother. I am taking away any and all magic you received as such. Once I touch you, all that you had, all that I gave you in the form of magic and longevity, is no longer yours to use. The things you stole from the fae are now on your head. The deaths of Rosemary and her son Sorrel are not your fault solely. You are related to me no more, by the law of the fae." He watched his brother as his words sunk into his mind. Before he could say anything, even had he anything to say, his body began the process of aging. "You will now be dust, so your remains will be cast out and put to sea, so you will never rise again with any magic."

The screams could have been heard for miles, Basil was sure. When Remi put her hand onto his arm, he could feel the power surging into her. It wasn't gentle either, the hold or the magic, but he stood there while she got everything that was for her to use.

"By order of the king of all fae, Juniper Herb, you are hereby sentenced to death. You will pay for your crimes by becoming no more." Juniper was suddenly nothing more than skin wrinkled around bones, his heart slowly pumping the last of its life-giving blood.

His beating heart was then lifted from his

body and destroyed by Remi. She did nothing but squeeze it tightly in her fingers before it was nothing more than particles of dust that fell to the earth rather than fly away on a breeze. Then his head was removed, and his skull crushed beneath her booted foot. The removal was complete. The same ritual had been performed on Rosemary's body earlier. It would be as he had said. Neither Juniper nor Rosemary would ever be able to rise again in a faerie circle.

Basil didn't know what he expected from the crowd, but cheering and happiness would never have been on his list. They were beyond thrilled with the events, he thought and wondered how much more he'd missed while being king. When people came to him, thanking him for a job well done, he tried hard to make sure everyone knew that he was no longer their king. They didn't seem to care about that either and greeted the new couple with hardy handshakes and hugs.

"That really wasn't a trial." He grinned at Alma. It had been a very long time since he'd seen her. "Not that it didn't end as it should have, but as for trials, that one sucked. How are you, Basil?"

"I'm wonderful now that I've found your son and daughter-in-law. They're a magnificent couple." He kissed Alma on the cheek and stepped back. "Alma?"

"Yes, we are mates. I've known for some time now. It's your smell, you see. When Harlin came to see you, I would smell your scent on him and knew what it meant. To think that we both went a different path and still ended up together." She laughed a little. "I guess the fates, they knew what they were about. I'd not have Harlin as my child had we gotten together long ago. Don't you think? You do want to be my mate, don't you?"

"Yes. Yes, and yes more." They were both laughing, and it occurred to him that they'd been speaking in fae. When he turned to Harlin, he knew then that he was well versed in the language and decided he'd have to remember that in the future. "Do you mind so much, my king? That I have your mother as my mate?"

"So long as you understand that I'd not hesitate a moment to do worse to you than anything anyone has ever done to his victims." Basil shivered. "I'm very happy for you both. You deserve a lot of happiness. Later we'll talk about this couple thing you were talking about. I'm assuming it's something extraordinary?"

"You have no idea."

They were both laughing as he and Alma walked away from the couple. They held hands as they spoke to people. They asked a lot of questions of him, and when he didn't have an answer, Alma did. It was wonderful, he thought, having someone at his side that didn't take swipes at the people they were around. Alma didn't even mind when people hugged her.

It was nearing midnight when the crowd started to disburse. He'd connected with a great many friends he'd not seen in some time, and he was able to be with Alma. They'd made a lot of decisions when they were alone tonight, and he was as happy as he'd ever been. They were going to find them a home tomorrow, one close to the kids, and he was excited to start the next chapter of his life with her.

He was headed to bed for the last time in the castle when a whisper of his name floated from down the hall toward him.

"Hello, Basil." He didn't see the person until they stepped out of the shadows. "I cannot stay here long, but I wanted to wish you well in your new life. The fates have given me this time to assure you from my own mouth that Sorrel wasn't your son. I am both glad and sad about that."

"Rosemary, how are you here?" She told him again that she'd been granted this special boon to tell him about Sorrel. "Thank you for that. I know you said it in the letter, but it was difficult for me to bear."

"I never loved you, not like I should have. I don't think I even loved Juniper like I should have. You are lucky to be able to find love now. Alma is a good woman." He nodded and told her he hadn't been this in love either. Rosemary laughed. "I'm sorry. That came out wrong."

"No, it was just right. You never loved me either. Which is good. It will be easier for you to move on now." She looked to her right, and he did as well. There was nothing there for him to see, but Rosemary nodded and looked at him. "I have one more gift for you. You don't have to worry about it harming you, but it is there in your room."

"Thank you again. I wish we could have at least parted in a better way. Did you enjoy your life with Juniper?" She didn't answer him, and he thought that was right too. "I'll miss you, Rosemary. I truly will."

"You were too good of a man for me. I should have seen that before. You were the best there was in all that you did." Again, he thanked her. "I must go. You and Alma will be happy. I know that."

Then she was gone. He moved into his bedroom, careful of where he was stepping. He realized then that he didn't trust Rosemary even after death. Striding to his bed, determined to forget the way she had come to him, he nearly flopped into the bed. A soft mewing sound came to him as he jerked back the covers.

The baby. It was just a tiny little thing staring up at him as hard as he was her. When she smiled at him, he could see that she was full of magic too. Her tiny body seemed to be vibrating from it. Picking her up, he knew she was fae, and that was when he found the note attached to her little outfit.

"Her name is Pixie. Please raise her as your own, as both her parents are dead. She needs good parents such as yourself." The note wasn't signed, but he knew it wasn't from Rosemary. She could neither read nor write. Pulling the little blanket off Pixie, he laughed when he saw her markings. She was indeed fae.

~*~

Remi didn't know what to think about the

castle she was to live in with Harlin. It was cold and drafty. There didn't seem to be any kind of indoor plumbing. Nor did she like that the kitchen wasn't a part of the place, but a stone building out back that was much too small for her tastes.

"My lady? If you would allow me to see what you have in mind for this place, I can make it better. I can see that you're upset." She nodded to Snow, the faerie that had been following her around since she entered the building. "You are unhappy with it all?"

"Yes, that pretty much sums it up. There is nothing here to make it worth not ripping it down and starting over." She knew she'd shocked the little creature, but she didn't care. "How are we supposed to keep warm when the weather turns cold? None of the fireplaces have proper ventilation. There isn't any way to go to the kitchen and grab a snack when I want. I'd have to walk out in the weather to not just get something to eat but to take a shit as well. Who designed this mess? A hermit that had no needs beyond a roof over his head?"

"I don't know who that might be or who would be living here without your permission, my lady." She growled and scared Snow more.

"Just allow me to fix one thing for you, and we can work on the hermit. I will find him and set him out if that is what you wish."

Thinking about how explaining to her what a hermit was would take too long. Instead, she told her that she wanted electricity in the whole place. Snow only stared at her, and Remi had to count to ten five times before she could explain what she needed her to do.

"I want you to go to Piper and Grant's castle. See how it's made. Spend some time there getting a good picture of what I want. In fact, look around there and come back here and make this castle like theirs. That way, once we get that portion of it fixed up, we can work on the other things."

Snow smiled, snapped her fingers, and left her. Remi went to find Harlin. It looked like he was having difficulty too.

"No, I'm not unhappy about the greenhouse. I'm not happy with the way it's designed. You need to start over with this one, and we'll begin again." Whoever he was talking to was too small for her to see from where she was. Getting closer, she could see that there were two brownies sitting on the stone waiting for him to tell them what the hell he was talking about. He looked at her, and she could see his frustration all over his body. "I can't make them understand me."

"I can fix that." She put out her hand, and they came to her. "There is a greenhouse behind Lord Grant's home. Have you seen it?" They both nodded. "Good. I want you to make this one look like that one, with all the running water and walls here. Only larger. Ten times—"

Harlin interrupted her. "No, not ten times. The same size for now. That way, if it's still not what I'm looking for, I can add on as we work. All right?" They disappeared the same way Snow had. "Is it going well for you? I have been out here for the last forty-five minutes trying to explain to them that this system no longer works for what we will be producing. I had no idea the faeries and the brownies were here to serve our kind, did you?"

"Not until today when Snow showed up with her crew. I didn't have any more luck making her understand either. I sent her to Piper's home to figure it out." They were both laughing when he pulled her into his arms. "I did go over the handbook this morning. It's like reading a book written in several languages, then translated into this one. It's currently being worked on with my magic to go back to the original one and work from there. That should help me get a handle on what the hell it is that I'm working with."

When Harlin kissed her, they walked hand in hand to the gardens behind their castle. It was magic too. Instead of using the land on one level, someone had stacked layer after layer of land atop one another to grow many things at one time. When there was a need for whatever was on the top, a person only had to touch that layer, and it would come to the ground level for you to pick from. There were saplings growing in the same kind of ground system too.

"You'd think if they were able to make this work, a simple thing like having running water and electricity would be an easy thing for them." Harlin told her this had been the working system here forever. But to them, electricity and indoor plumbing were still new. "I suppose. I do remember when we had to learn how to put on clothing. It was a nightmare for a while. We never got the hang of wearing a corset. I thought them to be stupid, but society back then required women to be in one. We compromised on it, I guess you could say, and only made our bodies look like we were in one."

He was still laughing when they came upon Basil and his mom. They were holding a bundle, and Remi wondered what they were doing. It wasn't until the baby started fussing that she realized they had a baby with them. Basil handed the little girl to her, then asked them to have a seat. He explained what had happened last night and how he was going to raise the little girl with Alma.

"That's wonderful. I wonder where she came from." Remi put her hand on the little girl's heart and found out everything she could about her. Looking up at the older couple, she was so happy she could help them with this. "Mother Earth said you are to raise her. She's the one that put her in your bed so you'd find her. Pixie's parents are indeed dead. They were killed by her for misdeeds done to her kind. I do know the child was considered an innocent and has been given all that was left behind by her parents. There wasn't much left. There is a house not far from where we are, and that is yours to keep her in. Mother Earth is hoping you'll wish to take on other children like this one that only needs good and loving parents to show them right from wrong. I have to say this is sort of freaking me out, the kind of shit I'm getting from a single touch."

They all laughed, and she looked at the little girl. There wasn't an ounce of meanness in her from her parents. While she knew the reason they had gotten this little girl now, Remi saw no reason for her new parents to know. Pixie's biological parents deserved to die and so much more, but she'd not been in charge of that part of Pixie's life.

They all played with her. She seemed to be about three months old and was enjoying the attention she was getting. It wasn't until Harlin took Pixie in his arms that she realized this was going to be his little sister. Remi glanced at Alma when she cleared her throat.

"I was worried you'd not take it well to have a sister so young." Harlin said he didn't care so long as she was happy. "I am too. Thank you for that, son. I am very happy. We've been looking for ourselves a home close to you, but if the one this child has is close, I see no reason for us not to enjoy it. Don't you think?"

Basil kissed Alma on the mouth when she turned to him. "I think it's a splendid idea, my dear. Splendid. We'll have all the makings of a big family before too much longer, and this little one will be able to play with her niece or nephew when they come along."

Again, Remi hadn't thought of that. Putting her hand over her still flat belly, she thought of her own child growing up around here. It had been a wonderful place for her, and she was sure that Harlin had had a good life here as well. Snow joined them just as they were deciding they were in need of something to eat. The lunch hour had long since passed.

"I believe I have it, my lady. Yes, I think so." They were headed to the house when both of the brownies Harlin had been working with caught up with them. "I'll show them the house, Jack and Jill, then I will let you show them the greenhouse. This is a wonderful day, I think, to have someone so interested in what can be done again." Snow looked at Basil. "I am sorry, my lord. I didn't mean that the way it sounded. But you have been ill for a very long time."

"No need to be sorry, Snow. I know I let things slide. I'm better now, and I'm hoping you can find someone to help me bring my home with my mate up to standards too." She said she knew just the person. "Good. No time like the present if you ask me. Let us go and see the house. I'm excited to see what changes have been made to it."

Remi was almost too afraid to look. When it was pointed out that the kitchen building was going to be used for storage, she headed there first. It had walls now, thick ones. There were several lights around, and she could see that shelving had been added to hold things.

"There is power, what it is called, running to the building now. There is room for many things to be put inside to keep fresh. I spoke with Mandy at the other house, and she explained to me how to make it so that fresh things would not freeze, but things that needed to be frozen will be taken care of that way. Magic is very nice for something like this, she told me, or we'd have to have many such buildings to keep things around for eating." Remi told her she liked that idea. "I'm glad, my lady. It was very good of you to send me to the other house. I was able to learn a great deal from there."

Walking into the back of the castle, they were stepping into what she thought of as a mudroom. There were shelves on each side of the wall, and it looked to her like someone had mentioned that shoes could be placed under the small bench. She was happy to see her shoes there and that someone had shined them up for her. They left that area to step into the kitchen.

"This is it, Snow. I can see me working in here." She walked around the room, touching the surfaces that were as smooth as stone. Remi realized that they were stones and that they had been used instead of anything else to work from.

In the center of the room was a long butcher's block, made of wood of every kind she'd ever seen. Remi knew it was from her sister, Blaze, and cherished it all the more for her thoughtfulness.

The two refrigerators side by side were stainless steel, and she loved that there would be plenty of room for anyone to enjoy food from them. Opening up the one closest to her, she was so happy to see that they'd filled it with things she was beginning to crave. Taking out a bottle of juice, she drank it straight down and grabbed another one to walk around with.

It wasn't just the kitchen that had been improved, but the entire house. Gone was the long room that she could see serving no purpose, but now was a part of the open area that led to the living room. A large fireplace was the replacement for the pit in the middle of the room that had terrified her on so many levels about someone falling into it. She knew that they'd have fun sitting in this room for decades to come. As soon as they found some furniture.

The other rooms had been redone too. The dining room, a place she knew would need to be large to hold their growing families, spilled out onto a covered walkway that had wisteria growing in long vines that nearly touched the ground. There was a large fire ring that could hold a cord of wood and warm the place for hours on end. The view, one she'd never get enough of, looked out over the sea, and even as late as it was, she could hear the frogs making their sounds, along with all the faeries out closing up the blooms that needed to be sheltered from the evening.

Their bedroom was the last one they checked out. The same view from the dining room was echoed from their windows, as well as the back yard and the mountain tops behind. As she was staring out the window, thinking of all the beauty that was now hers to look at, Harlin wrapped his arms around her from behind.

"I can tell that you like it. But you should say something to Snow before she explodes. She's looking a little worried." Remi did just what he asked her to do and told Snow she loved every part of the house and grounds around their new home. "Now we have to go and see what we have in the way of a greenhouse. I can only hope it's half as lovely as you are. Then I'll be set for life."

Another kiss, and they went to the place where the greenhouse was to be put in. As they moved closer to it, Remi could tell that there were changes going to be made on it. Not that Jack and Jill didn't get it right, but to work on the scale they were planning, there would be a need for stronger water flow, as well as more room.

"I still need to speak to the two of you about what you are." Remi nodded as Jill explained to Harlin what they were doing. Basil cleared his throat, then continued. "It's really important, Remi. I think the sooner you know what will happen, the better."

"I know. But for today, I just want to bask in the newness of this all. If this were to go all to shit tomorrow, I'd at least have this memory to sustain me. All right?" He nodded, but she could tell that Basil wanted to get his part in this finished. "I promise you, Basil, we'll talk to you first thing in the morning at breakfast. All right?"

"Yes. So long it's first thing. Yes, we'll be here for breakfast." She asked Alma what was going on as Basil made sure Harlin was sure about the meeting. She said she didn't know but would find out.

"Thank you for that. I think the more information we have beforehand, the better we'll be able to handle things." She asked her if she'd found the book of bylaws. "I have, but it's been translated too many times for me to figure out. I'm going to—"

"Just put your hand on it and ask to know them." Remi asked her if it would be understandable then. "Yes. You know fae and any other language that it might have notes in, but you only need to ask it to help you, and it will. Everything will help you. Even the soil we're standing on. I'm sure that will give you more than even Basil will be able to tell you."

"Thank you. I will do that as soon as we leave here." She looked at the greenhouse, then back at her mother-in-law. "Are you happy, Alma? I mean, very happy?"

"I'm happier than I've ever been, child. I promise you. And having you mated to my son gives me so much more happiness that I can't put it to words." She hugged her. "You're wonderful for this old woman. I want you to know that I'm here for you, either of you, whenever you need me."

Chapter 6

Harlin wasn't sure he wanted to hear anymore, but Remi was looking a little bit pissy, so he tried his best to pay attention. But what she was telling him and what he wanted to believe were two different things entirely. Like he knew he was going to live forever and not be killed, but to know that there was nothing manmade or magical that could even harm him was a little too much to take in.

"Are you listening to me?" He nodded, then shook his head. "What the fuck is that supposed to mean? Either you are, or you're not. I'm not going to explain this all to you again and have you asking me what I said. Again. Listen to the words coming out of my mouth."

"I am. I don't understand them right now. Not that you're talking gibberish, but I'm taking this the best way I can. To know some of the things—are you sure we can stay underwater indefinitely? I mean, what the hell would that help?" She told him. "Okay, I guess it would be good to be able to look and see what is down there, but why would I care? Do you?"

"Yes, as a matter of fact, I do care. What if I was looking for a body or something that was hidden away? Don't you think it would be better in finding it rather than waiting around for a diving team to get geared up and such before we knew?" She glared at him. "Here is one that I just thought of and realized it wouldn't happen. I could stuff you in a cave and hope you drown when the sea waters come in. You don't need to have a way to use the shit I'm telling you, Harlin, only that you can do it. There are millions of things that could go shit up, and some of this might come in handy. But to sit here and give you a reason you might need to use it is going to take all fucking night. I'm exhausted. You said you wanted information before Basil got here. Well, I'm trying to give it to you."

"This is the way I work." She told him to work someplace else and to let her tell him the rest. "I don't want to know anything else. I've decided it's just too much for us both to know, and you learned it. I'll turn to you when I need you."

"You're going to be shit out of luck when I'm the one doing this shit to you, and I have the answers but won't give them to you." He thought she was being terribly mean to him right now but grinned. She was certainly adorable when she—"Damn it, Harlin, I'm going to hurt you if you don't pay attention."

"I'm sorry. All right. Just tell me one thing at a time, and only the really important stuff. I'm overwhelmed if you want to know the truth. I'm sure you are as well, but I just need a few minutes before you give me too much more." She nodded. "How were you able to get this stuff anyway? Did the book finally pan out for you?"

"Mother Earth gave it to me." She snapped her fingers and sat up on her knees. "I can do that too, I just realized. I can make sure you have it while I'm not getting pissed off at you for trying to explain."

Before he could tell her that he liked her

way of doing things, she touched her fingers to his forehead. He heard her saying something, but it was blocked out by the information seemingly downloading in his mind. Everything suddenly became crystal clear. Not only that, but he had an understanding of being a fae much better than he had before. Looking at her, when his mind seemed to slow a bit, he watched her.

"You understand now why it was so important that he gave us the information. We'll be bombarded now with other kings wanting to take our kingdom away from us. Much like, from what I gathered, the men did to other castles when they were invaded. We'll need to take a stand from the very start and not fob it off as no real threat. It will put out there that we're too soft and that anyone can take this should they want." He asked her if she knew how to do that. To take a stand. "I do. I worked with Dante and the others on this sort of thing. What we need to do is establish a power when the first king arrives and let them see how we work shit out."

"So...." He wanted to have her tell him how to do it so he could keep her safe, but he also knew that even if he had all the knowledge she did now, he'd never be able to pull it off. Not without a great

many people and creatures they were taking care
of getting hurt. "You do what you need to do, and
I'll be right there with you. I'd ask that you don't
second guess yourself in thinking I need to be
involved. I would love to be, but I know nothing
of warfare and even less about having to take a
stand against a fleet of boats or whatever comes
here than I do about what to make for dinner for
the two of us."

The kiss on his mouth made him feel better.
However, it didn't lessen his worry about her
getting harmed. He loved her. Remi was his life.
And should anything happen to her or their babe,
Harlin didn't know what he'd do with himself.

"We can't get hurt. Remember that. Keep
telling yourself that over and over. We're too
powerful to get hurt. That doesn't mean we can't
be run out of the castle if we do this wrong, but
they can't harm us." Harlin told her he needed to
remember that. "Yes, you do. Now, I've called the
birds to let them know we'll need them to help
us and told them what I might need from them.
There is no point in keeping it a secret that we
have them when a great many lives are at stake.
All right?"

Only an hour had passed by the time they'd

worked out a plan to make sure that no one could take their castle and lands. They'd then go over it in the afternoon with the other birds to let them know what their parts were. When Basil arrived at seven after seven, Harlin felt that he was as prepared mentally as he was ever going to be. Basil sat down at the table, and without any kind of built-up, told him that someone had arrived to make war.

"So soon?" He nodded. Then he bowed his head. "We're ready for whoever comes this way, Basil. We're prepared and can defend almost any place surrounding us."

When the earth shook, even the stone floor he was standing on, he knew the birds in all their glory had arrived. The faeries and fae, along with all manner of smaller creatures, came into the castle keep. He looked at the birds when he went to the yard and thought he'd run as fast as he could in the other direction if they were someone he had to fight in battle.

"Are you ready?" Instead of answering her with babbling, as he was sure would happen, he kissed Remi on the mouth and held her hand to his heart. "We've got this. Mercy knew the first candidate had arrived earlier this morning. She sent word out to all the other people around to keep hidden in their homes. Also, Duncan has given us his army of faeries to use as a backup. We're not just an army to reckon with, Harlin, but a force to behold."

He knew that too and let out the long breath he'd been holding. Walking to the now open gates of their castle grounds, he saw the troll with his own army seemed thrilled that they were coming out to greet him.

"So you're just going to lay down your arms and give in to me. I like that in a way. Takes a great deal of fun out of it for me and my men, but I do like it when a person knows they are defeated right at the beginning. I will make provisions for your—"

"I'm sorry. Why would you think such a thing from us?" Harlin didn't know where his bravado was coming from at the moment, but he was glad he was able to speak to the man. "We're only out here to find out who we should notify as your next of kin when you are beheaded. You do know when you come to a land that has been claimed by a king and queen, the person who tries to take it is to be killed. Are you? Are you ready to be beheaded?"

"Of course not." The troll looked at his men and women lined up behind him. They were armed with large trees as battering rams. Pick hammers that seemed bigger than Harlin was. When the troll laughed again, he looked directly at Remi. "I heard that you are with child, Lady Remi. It would be a shame to have to harm you and your child today. Why don't you toddle on home and let the men take care of this? You'll be safe from harm until after the child is born."

"How nice of you. What will you do with my child after you have me murdered, Timothy the Troll? Will you have it for your dinner, as you have other queens' children?" Remi laughed. Then she took a step forward and looked directly at Timothy as she lifted from the ground with her new wings. "You can end this now and live to see another day if you turn back the way you've come and leave us to our home."

"That isn't going to happen." He took a step, and the earth rumbled around them. "You will all die this day if you stand with him."

Harlin felt the brush of wings when the first bird flew over them. The shadow that was left in her wake made him think it was Mercy. When she landed in the field to the troll's right, Blaze as her hawk landed on the other side of him.

They were all there, their beautiful deadliness for anyone to see. Their claws were as big as houses. Their wings were spread out far and wide. The other two, the owl and the phoenix, made him proud to be a part of this day. And his fear of anyone dying also lessened as they squawked and yelled at the troll's army.

"You have birds, I see. Such puny things if you ask me. Is this a trick of magic? Are you trying to scare me with your showing of birds so large? It will not work. So that you know, I am stronger than any magic you have around you." Piper blew white-hot flames at the men behind Timothy, killing more than half his men. "You would dare do such a thing to me? To kill my men even before the battle has begun? Unfair. I take your castle yonder for what you have done to me this day."

"And what of the twenty-four faeries you murdered on your way here? You cannot tell me that you had no idea they were about. They flew at your head the entire time, trying to warn you that you were on their land, their homeland. You murdered my people even before you showed yourself to be an ass to us. What of that?" Timothy said he had no idea what she was speaking of. "I'm sure you'd like me to believe that, but I don't. Would you like to speak to someone that knows all?"

Mother Earth showed herself before them. Harlin wanted to bow before her, but Remi held him upright. With a snap of her fingers, the dead, all of them, were laid out before the troll. The injured were being helped by the other faeries. It sickened him to think that so much had already been done, and they were still talking to this man.

"You have done this for no other reason than you could. I will take a penance from you, Timothy the Troll. And you will not fight me on this." Mother Earth disappeared, and the dead did as well. When Harlin looked at Timothy again, he was missing an eye as well as an arm. Another portion of his men were missing as well.

"You are diminished by a great deal, Timmy boy. How on earth do you expect to take us on without the army you once had, as well as missing your parts? I'm sure if you look, your twig and berries have been removed as well. You can no longer produce heirs such as yourself. Thank you, Mother Earth, for that." Timothy looked into his pants. While he didn't know what he was looking at, he could tell that what Remi had said to him was a fact. He looked around as if he were looking for them. "Missing, are they? Well, I, for one am happy to know that. To think that there could be more than just you running around is a little sickening. Especially since there will be no one there to tell them the story as to how you lost your life. You will, you know. I plan on having your head removed soon. Do you have any last words? Anything to say before you're dead?"

"You are fighting unfairly." Harlin laughed and asked him how he thought that was true. "You have taken a good portion of my men. But that isn't the bad part. It's that you took away my manhood. I had a great and large one, and you have had it removed by magic."

"I believe you heard the Mother say it was payment." He shook his head and said it was too much. "Shall I bring her back here for you to tell her that? I can. You just say the word, and she'll be right here."

"No. No. I do not wish to bother her. She will only get angry that she's been caught in her mistake and perhaps take more of me. No, we shall leave it alone for another time." He was afraid of the Mother of the Earth, and rightly so, he thought. "I will need to come back another time. It seems I have forgotten about another fight I was to take on."

"No. You will end it here." Timothy asked Remi what she'd do if he left. "You will never see the sunset again, for I shall kill you where you stand. I'm going to anyway, but you're not leaving here without you being dead. Your men too. You should have listened to your mate when she told you it was too dangerous for you to come here so soon after we'd taken the job. Now you will leave her alone for no other reason than you're stupid."

The pick hammer in his hand started to move. Timothy was drawing it back so as to more than likely slam it down onto their heads. Standing still, awaiting the blow, Harlin heard the whistle of wings flying quickly, then nothing at all. Opening his eyes, Harlin took in the scene before him.

Timothy was the only one standing upright. His heart had been burnt through with a flame hot enough to not leave much in the way of open wounds. It looked like his body was being held up only by the strength of his legs and the hammer that was propped against his leg. As his head rolled back and off the shoulders on which it had been all these years, the faeries began their job of cleaning up. Not a single piece of the trolls would be there by evening.

The other trolls were dead, their heads near their bodies, with the green ooze of their kind seeping into the earth. The weapons they had brought with them, nothing more than trees and some metal things that Harlin figured they'd stolen from other kingdoms, were put aside to be broken down and used for something else.

Duncan showed up just as Timothy's head was being pulled away and taken apart for things to be used for the other animals. "Are you all right?" Harlin told him he wasn't sure just yet. "I heard what you did here. You've done well. My mother would have been very proud of you both."

"I thought we were dead a couple of times. No matter how many times someone tells you that you won't die, you can't help but think they might have it wrong. This didn't last nearly as long as I thought it would." Duncan looked out over the dead still being dealt with. "Remi said the story of what happened here will be spread wide and far. It will be a good long time before anyone tries this again. Do you suppose she's right?"

"No. There'll be others. I think she was only

telling you that so you'd rest easier. You were here when my mother was alive. You got your memories back. How many times did it take for others to still not get it in their head that they were nothing compared to what she was?" He had forgotten about that. Or he wanted to. "It's a good thing the dragons are friends of the earth, or that would have been a good deal harder to clean up today. I saw Piper as I was coming here. She is so happy to have been able to be helpful again. She said that when the faeries and such got all they wanted, she'd burn the fields to the earth for you. That's a wonderful idea."

Harlin walked with Duncan so he could find Remi. She was still out on the field directing things to be taken away, the rest of it to be burned. He smiled at her when she waved at him. Having her at his side, he was happier now than he'd ever been at any time in his life.

~*~

By nightfall, the dead were taken care of, and the ground was already showing signs of recovery. No one could eat the meat of a troll, but the skin was very useful to all manner of small animals. It would be stretched out and dried for roofs of houses for them. Also, the bones, since they were so hard, could be sharpened and used for saws and knives that all creatures needed. Remi stopped to watch a group of brownies trying their best to take care that their bounty wasn't lost on their way home. The hair of the troll, while not a great deal of it, would be used for sewing things like sails on boats, as well as chopped up in brews for a salve that would heal almost any kind of cuts. Picking up the brownies' things, she took them to their workshop so that they'd not have to strain themselves any longer.

"You have done well here today. I hope you know how much they all appreciate it." She knew who was speaking to her but didn't bother looking for her. Dante had been visiting her for several days now. "Are you now glad that I made you into what you are?"

"I was never unhappy about being a bird for you. Never that. I didn't care for being a human, not until lately. What I was upset with you about was how you'd gone about it. There was no reason for you to die like you did. Not telling us that you were taking a poison that would make it so you'd feel nothing. That is why I'm upset with you." She said she hadn't thought anyone would care. "That's bullshit, and you know it. Everyone loved you, and every one of us would have died for you or with you."

"I know that now." She turned and saw the misty figure of her queen. "You can see me now because you are so very powerful. More so than even my Duncan. You and Harlin will be able to keep everyone safe for decades to come while improving the way the lands are cared for. I knew you'd fall in love with Harlin. What I didn't know was what you'd bring to each other in the way of magical power. You are more than I ever thought possible for one of my birds."

"I never wanted to be without you. Although I knew Mercy was your favorite, I also knew I loved you more than she did. And in a different way. My love for you was like a daughter to a mother. Not friend to friend, as she loved you." Dante told her she'd not known that. "I'm sure that even though you have the gift of sight, my dear queen, there is plenty you didn't know about."

"I knew you would go into the trees and fell things for the families to have. Seeds from trees, pinecones for the children to decorate for gifts at Christmas. That you give a bit of yourself to small animals, just enough that they'd be healed from whatever ailed them. They were to still die, but with their family around and not some bear attack where no one would find their bodies. You also fished for the families that had no means to do so. Filled a net nearly as big as you with fresh meat for families too proud to ask for help. You also took care that there were funds for kids that wished to leave the area. One by one, they'd leave, only to return and add to the bounty that is here now. You did all that without anyone knowing it." Remi told her she liked to do those things. "Do you? I also know that as a human, you made sure that each of your employees in every restaurant you had was well paid and well-fed. When you had to shut down one of them years ago because of a fire, I believe you paid them all, even using some of your own funds to make sure they were all right."

"I had plenty enough that I knew I would never starve." Dante told her it was more than that. "Don't rehash things in order to soften me up for something, Dante. Just tell me what it is so you can go back to your deathly slumber."

"I know you say that not to be mean, but you wish me to rest so I can see my son more. I don't visit him as much as he'd like for me to. It's not good that he would come to me so often now that he has a mate. What of your mate, Remi? Where is he?" She told her what she knew. "That's right. Your quiet giant is out making sure the families of the fallen today have enough to make up for the loss. He is also telling them how their bravery in making sure the others were hidden away is all that saved them. Harlin is a good man."

"He is. I love him very much." Dante sat on the stone beside her. Her body was just a mist right now, but enough so that Remi could make out her face if she looked hard enough. "Do you know what my child will be, Dante? Will he be strong like his father. Smart too?"

"He will be everything to you both, and that is all that matters. The child you have next will be a handful for you, but you will handle her well enough. She will be exactly like you in all things. A great warrior, as well as a woman compassionate for the next part of her life."

"I know nothing of children and rearing them. I'm glad to have the help of Alma beside me so I can not mess up too badly." Dante told her she'd not mess up at all if she only loved them. "I do already. Even though he's not shown himself to be here yet, I still find myself ready for him to come into the world."

Dante left her a while later. She couldn't stay long, not on this side of death, and Remi was glad she'd left on a good note this time. The other times she'd come to see her had ended in a fight or cross words. Today was different. Dante wasn't mean to her, but there were things Remi didn't want to hear from her. Like the fact that she couldn't come back too often, as it was not right for any of them to have her over their shoulder all the time. Remi had asked her why this time should be so different than any other time when she'd been alive, and that pissed the queen off. She'd left in a huff and Remi in tears. She so wished she could have a nice long conversation with her and it not end badly for either of them.

It was Alma that sat next to her this time. After handing her Pixie, Alma sat there for several minutes, not saying a word. It was fine by Remi — she didn't care for useless chatter anyway.

"Would you believe me if I told you that the queen from long ago came to see me just now?" Remi told her she'd believe anything she told her. "Thank you. But she told me you needed more than a friend. You needed a mother. I wasn't at all sure what she was talking about until I remembered you were never human when you were growing up. You missed a great deal, she told me."

"I did. I have. But I have also learned a great deal in my lifetime. More than I think you have living in that nursing home faking your own insanity. What was that like? Living there knowing you could be caught at any time?" She said it was frightening. "I bet it was. But I also think a great many of the residents benefited from you being there. How often did you come out of your room to feed and care for them?"

"You're too smart for your own good, young lady." Remi laughed and played with Pixie while Alma continued. "Daily. Sometimes I'd never get back to my room for days at a time, worrying about the others. The magic I had saved us all from starving to death. Meds, while I knew very little about them, I could figure out well enough. Some of the faeries that helped me, they did a great deal of the heavy work. Changing beds, bathing them and such. It wasn't until the last few months or so that I realized no one was coming to rescue us. That we were all on our own."

"You would have continued to help them and keep them safe." She nodded and said she would have. "I know nothing about babies, much less magical ones. I'd like you to help me with that. I'm sure you have a wealth of information to hand down to me."

"I think we'll be helping each other on that. I only realized today that I'm the mother of a man that is decades—no, centuries old, and I've been hiding him away from the world too." She looked at her, and Remi smiled. "You're good for my son, Remi. He loves you, of course, but you make him feel as if he were atop of the world all the time. That is all a mother could ask for her children. For them to find happiness."

"I do want that for my child. That and to be a good person. I spent enough time in the human world to know it's not always that way. A person could be raised to be good, and something happens, and it all goes to shit. I'm going to teach them, with Harlin, what is right and wrong, and hope for the very best. I think you'd agree with me on that." Alma said she did. "I know you have your own house, but I do hope you'll come to see us a great deal. Stay with us too."

"I was hoping you'd say that." They hugged, and Pixie went to Alma. "She'll make the two of us young, Basil and I. We've both fallen in love with her so hard in just this little bit of time. We were asked to see if we'd like to take on other children like Pixie here. Children abandoned for one reason or another."

"That will be wonderful. I heard from one of the faeries yesterday that the house for abused children is full up again. So many of them being hurt for no good reason. I don't understand that myself." Alma said she didn't either but had been helping out as much as she could. "I'm going to help as well. Maybe after this child is born, Harlin and I can bring a few of them here to live and be a part of our family. Perhaps before that."

"I'm sure they'd welcome you to do that for them." Alma stood up. "I've much to do now that I feel better. Sometimes I have missed that. Just talking to someone that has no vested interest in not telling me the truth when I ask for it. I'd very much like to meet with you more if that is all right with you."

"It is. Every Wednesday night is the night my sisters and I get together." Alma told her she'd not bother her on those nights. "That's not why I told you. I want you to join us. The more, the merrier, I think. We never have our cell phones or computers but talk and argue a great deal about everything. I think you might well enjoy that too."

"I think I'd love that. Thank you."

Remi nodded, and Alma left with Pixie. Getting up, she went to find Harlin. She wanted him to take her to bed and never get out of it again—not practical, but it was a good try, she thought. Finding him with Basil and the brownies at the greenhouse, she left them to it and went to find Esme. Her mate might even be here now, she thought, and that would be a blast for all of them.

Laughing, Remi thought she was lucky to have found Harlin when she did. All of them had their mates come to them when they were needed most. Mercy had been about to have a nervous breakdown was the one thing Remi remembered the most about her having a mate around. Not only had Joel calmed her down, but he loved her with all he was. And loving Mercy was not an easy task. Yes, she thought again, she was happy to have all her family here, and all of them in love. She wondered what sort of person Esme would find to love.

AWARD WINNING, BESTSELLING AUTHOR

Kathi Barton, a winner of the Pinnacle Book Achievement Award and a best-selling author on Amazon and All Romance books, lives in Nashport, Ohio, with her husband, Paul. When not creating new worlds and romance, Kathi and her husband enjoy camping and going to auctions. She can also be seen at county fairs with her husband, who is an artist and potter.

Her muse, a cross between Jimmy Stewart and Hugh Jackman, brings her stories to life for her readers in a way that has them coming back time and again for more. Her favorite genre is paranormal romance, with a great deal of spice. You can visit Kathi online and drop her an email if you'd like. She loves hearing from her fans. aaronskiss@gmail.com.

Follow Kathi on her blog: http://kathisbartonauthor.blogspot.com/